PIONEER BLISS

THE O'ROURKE FAMILY MONTANA SAGA, BOOK FIVE

RAMONA FLIGHTNER

GRIZZLY DAMSEL PUBLISHING

Jefe
I'll never forget your eyes gleaming with
delight as you told me your
latest brilliant idea.
Thank you for being my greatest cheerleader.

CHAPTER 1

Missouri River, Late May 1867

"**E**veryone down!"
The captain's voice rang loud and clear, as arrows pelted the side of the steamboat and as the *ping* of bullets against the boiler-plated pilothouse echoed in the otherwise quiet riverbed area. Declan O'Rourke launched himself at the nearby young woman, hauling her down and covering her with his broad shoulders and back. He would not allow anything to happen to her.

He shivered as he heard the *whoops* of delight as the Indians charged, their horses' hooves thundering over the riverbank, as they approached the docked steamboat. Shattered glass sprinkled over Declan, as the Indian's bullets landed too close for comfort.

Declan glanced up and noted he was at a door, leading into the dining area and staterooms. Squirming around until he could kick it, he battered at it until it crashed open. "Hold on," he murmured, a moment before he yanked the prostrate woman off the ground and unceremoniously pushed her inside. He slammed the door shut, pulled her to the farthest side of the room, and toppled over a small table for them to hide behind.

The sound of guns firing continued to echo throughout the riverbed, although it sounded as though the majority were fired from the men on the steamboat, rather than the marauders on land. After a hair-raising cry, Declan heard horses stampeding away. A heavy stillness settled over the steamboat, the quiet interrupted as men swore, glass crinkled underfoot, and a few men called out for aid. Others laughed and began the retelling, already exaggerating their role in rebuffing the Indian attack. Hoping there were men on board who could help the injured, Declan focused on the woman in his arms.

Staring into her terror-filled eyes, he demanded, "Tell me he's well. That he's unharmed." When she remained unresponsive and shivering, his hands ran over the bundle tied securely against her chest. Only when the baby gave a small squeal of delight, as though the entire adventure had been exhilarating rather than terrifying, did Declan heave out a breath of relief. "Thank God. The lad's well."

His words seemed to finally stir her from her stupor, and she nodded. Her arms had remained wrapped around the baby throughout it all, and she kissed his head. "Yes, he's well. As am I."

"Good," Declan muttered. "I don't know where I'd find another wet nurse en route to Montana Territory." He grimaced, as he knew he sounded ungrateful for all she had done for him. "I'm glad you're well, Samantha. I didn't mean—" He broke off what he would have said with a sigh. Once, he had been known for his charm. Now he feared he would always be a bitter, surly man.

"I understand. Your concern will always be for him. As it should be." She shifted, reminding him that he remained half on top of her. "I believe the threat is gone, sir."

"Aye, it is." He heard the captain, bellowing for men to haul in timber for the steam engine. "Although I wouldn't put it past the Indians to attempt another attack while we're docked again." He pushed away and stood, offering his hand for her to rise. When she was on her feet, he peered at the bundle resting against her chest. "How's my lad?" he murmured, running a finger down the boy's cheek. At the babe's gurgle and a smile, Declan felt a tightness in his chest ease. "Here. Let me hold him."

2

Samantha loosened the bindings of the wrap she had fashioned to hold the baby in place and slipped him into Declan's arms. "I'll need to feed and to change him soon."

"I know," he murmured, breathing in the soft scent of the baby. "I want a moment with him." He kissed one silky cheek and then the other. "He might not need soothing, but I do. And you're a good lad, aren't you?" he said to his son. "Calmin' down your da." He ran a hand over the babe's satiny smooth head before kissing it too. Stepping outside to the opposite side of the steamboat, away from the riverbank and any possibility of a stealth attack, he faced the Missouri River. "Ah, lad, you have no idea how much joy you've brought me."

At his son's gurgle, Declan chuckled, cradling him against his chest. Even though he stared at the muddy ever-churning waters of the mighty Missouri, he failed to see the elevated riverbank or the swallows swooping, as they built their nests in the cliffs. Instead he saw *her*. The beautiful, deceitful Magnolia Harding.

The room was smoky, with the lamplight casting an eerie, yet romantic light over the ballroom. Men prowled as they looked over the women, who stood to the side of the room, preening and posturing. Men outnumbered women, and the women knew they would have their choice of dance partners this evening. With a sigh, Declan resigned himself to another tedious evening of watching his younger brothers, Eamon and Finn, flirt and cajole women with their charm and sweet words.

After accepting a glass of watered-down whiskey, he stood, arrested in place at the sight of the most beautiful woman he had ever beheld. Gold curls framed her face, while crystal clear blue eyes met his with an audacious boldness. Against his will, he pushed through the crowd, eager to hear if her voice was as sweet as she looked.

"Miss," he murmured, flushing at his inane beginning. "If you're not spoken for, would you dance with me?"

"I could never dance with a gentleman when I do not even know his name," she said in a soft, sultry voice, redolent of the antebellum South.

"I beg your pardon." Declan ran a hand through his thick black hair, then wiped his sweat-soaked palm on his pants. "I'm Declan O'Rourke."

"An Irishman," she murmured, unable to hide the slight disdain in her voice.

"Aye," Declan said. "I'm Irish, although I help run a prosperous business in Fort Benton, Montana Territory."

"Oh, I do enjoy an ambitious man."

Rocking back on his heels, he smiled at her. "Well, you won't find an O'Rourke who isn't ambitious." He paused. "Miss ... ?"

"Miss Harding," she said, as she reached out her arm. "And I do so love a waltz." She raised her eyebrows in a mocking manner. "You do know how to waltz."

Swallowing, Declan shrugged. "I can stumble my way through one, miss." He rested his hand over hers, gently tugging her with him to the makeshift dance floor. As he pulled her into his arms, he relished the feel of her against him and wished the moment never had to end.

A dustpan rattling with glass fragments jerked him from his reminiscence. Declan gripped the baby to his chest, kissing his head again, as wee Gavin gurgled with pleasure. "Ah, there's a good lad," he murmured. "Always content. Always happy."

He frowned as he considered Gavin's mother. The mercurial and mercenary Magnolia Harding. Although as beautiful as a confection, she had hid a cruelty and a selfishness that he had detected too late. "Almost too late," he murmured, as he rubbed his cheek over Gavin's head.

"Ye all right there, sonny?" the wiry captain called down to him from the uppermost deck surrounding the pilothouse. After a moment, clattering feet sounded on the steps, and the captain approached. A man of middling height, he had thick brown hair and dark-brown eyes that hid his keen awareness of all around him.

"I'm fine, sir." Declan smiled at the man who had taken an interest in him and his small entourage, since the moment he had boarded the steamboat weeks ago in Saint Louis.

"Your young'un all right?" He scratched at his head, sending a few strands on end. "I know there will be those bellyachin' you didn't come to fight, but we had plenty of men all too eager to let off some steam." He shook his head. "Don't let 'em get to you."

4

"Sir, thank you," Declan said.

"Now let me see that darlin' boy of yours. You know I never can have enough baby time." He grinned at Declan, who turned, so that Gavin faced the captain, a little bit of drool dribbling down his chin. "Will you come to Uncle A.J.?" He held out his arms, his smile flashing, when the baby made a sound of delight as Declan handed him over.

"Oh, I've got you, lad," the captain said. "I only wish my dear Bessie could see you. She'd spoil you rotten. But then your papa tells me that he's taking you home. To meet your grandparents. And your true aunts and uncles."

Declan made a sound of disagreement. "A child can never have too many people who care for him. I thank you for your regard for him, sir."

"Sir, sir. Don't go *sirring* me. I ain't your boss. Call me A.J. or Mr. Pickens. But I prefer A.J.," he said with a broad smile, as he rested his head against young Gavin's downy head. After another long moment, he gave a reluctant sigh. "I have to check on the rest of the crew and guests." He kissed Gavin's head. "'Til next time, little one." He handed Gavin back to Declan and moseyed away, calling out to crew and men loitering on the deck. Rather than groans at his approach, the men responded with laughter and good-natured ribbing.

Declan smiled, thankful for the captain's friendship. This was the third river trip Declan had taken—one to Fort Benton when his family moved there in 1863, and now the round trip river trip to and from Saint Louis—and none of the other captains had been person-able or interested in friendship with the people on board. Instead they'd been solicitous but distant, as though understanding the moments spent on the steamboat were fleeting and would lead to no lasting amity.

A.J. seemed unique. As far as Declan could tell, this captain knew every passenger's name and enjoyed talking with each of them, if he had time. He never partook in any gambling or excessive drinking but enjoyed watching others lose their shirts and their sobriety. A self-proclaimed romantic, he loved a good story. Declan feared A.J. waited to hear Declan's tale. "Well, you'll wait in vain," he muttered, as he nodded to Samantha, who shifted from foot to foot, as she kept an eye on her charge. With a reluctant sigh, he handed his son over to her, counting the minutes until he saw Gavin again.

~

A week later, they were only another week short of their arrival at Fort Benton. Declan had left Gavin with Samantha, as he strolled to the deck, determined to have a few moments to himself. Although he had thought his surliness—and the fact he was a single father traveling with a young woman—would deter any woman on the boat from approaching him, that had not been the case. So far, he'd had to dissuade each young woman on the vessel from their pursuit of him. Somehow they believed him to be a prosperous merchant. He grunted as he fingered his well- tailored suit, wondering why the trappings and appearance of wealth were all that were needed to provoke interest. Grimacing, he recalled that he, too, had once been drawn in by the superficial, without searching for substance.

He scoffed and let out a deep breath in an attempt to relax. The steamboat was docked in the middle of the Missouri, rocking slowly in place to the gentle sway of the large river. In this position, they were protected from any attacks, although they were more vulnerable to large pieces of driftwood floating downstream. However, after their recent Indian attack, A.J. wanted no further incidents that could delay their arrival at Fort Benton.

After another deep breath that failed to relax him, Declan swore softly. Nothing would relieve him of his mounting anxiety about returning home. Facing his family. Acknowledging to his father that he had been a fool. Ducking his head, he resented that he was returning a failure.

He dreaded seeing the disappointment in his mum's gaze. That thought alone nearly gutted him. However, he didn't know what to do or where else to go. The thought of remaining alone, with a baby, in

Saint Louis was past bearing. He wanted and needed his family around him. He couldn't imagine not sharing the joys of his son with someone. Anyone.

"You look as lonely as a tick wishin' for somethin' to bite," A.J. said, as he approached. "What's the matter, sonny?"

Declan smiled, as that seemed to be A.J.'s favorite question, at least with regard to him. "I'm envisioning my return home."

"Seems to make you *dyspeppered*," A.J. said, as he rocked his shoulder into Declan's.

"*Dyspeppered*?" Declan asked. "What sort of word is that?"

"Oh, a fine word. My Bessie, now, she's a librarian. And she knows all sorts of fancy words. She's lost patience with my inability to keep any of 'em straight." He laughed and slapped a hand onto the railing, as though he'd just told the finest joke. "So I told her, fine. I'll give you words. Big pompous words. And I have."

Declan gaped at him a moment, before a smile dawned. "You mean to tell me that you just make up words? Words that sound good to you?"

"You tellin' me that ain't a good-soundin' word?" A.J. asked, his eyebrows raised. "It's every bit as good as anythin' a doc would tell ye."

"*Dyspeptic*," Declan breathed. "Of course."

A.J. smiled at him, as though Declan were saying the same word. "So, sonny, is your family mean? Will they reject your son?"

Declan shook his head. "Of course not. They're wonderful." He shrugged, then shook his head again. "It's just that I wish I were coming home with a bride. Along with a son."

A.J. let out a wheezy sigh, as he pulled out his pipe. After tapping in tobacco, he lit it, while pulling in air to the pipe. When he was satisfied the pipe was lit, he threw the match into the water below. He gave a few pulls on his pipe, nodding with contentment, as the sweet, smoky scent of tobacco filled the air. "Now you tell me what's got you so riled up, sonny. Doesn't seem to be no good reason for it."

Declan sighed and rested one hip on the railing as he faced A.J. "You don't understand, sir." He spoke with the faintest hint of Ireland in his voice. "I was raised to believe I should not have children until I was married. And that my wife would be a good, respectable woman, who liked my family as much as I loved them." He shook his head. "I failed. And I dread seeing their disappointment."

A.J. puffed away at his pipe for long moments. Finally he lowered the pipe and tapped it in the air, as his brown eyes gleamed with sincerity. "I've seen how you dote over that boy. Seen how you love him. Protect him from all harm. Ain't no decent father or mother in the world who'll take exception to their son lovin' a child that way." He paused. "From what you've said, your folks are more than decent, sonny."

Flushing, Declan nodded. "Aye. They're wonderful."

"Then they ain't the problem. You are." He nodded as he drew on his pipe again, while meeting Declan's incredulous stare. "You've got puffed-up notions of who you are and what you're supposed to be. They're about chokin' the life out of you, son."

Declan glared at him with indignant anger.

"You know I'm right, an' it only makes ye ornerier." He smiled, his teeth clamped around his pipe. "*You* wish things was different. *You* wish you was comin' home with a bride your mama could be proud to call daughter. But you ain't. And now you're makin' up all sorts of fears in your head." He paused. "What was your woman like?"

"A deceitful witch," the younger man rasped, as he closed his eyes. "I risked my family for her."

Puffing on his pipe, A.J. nodded in commiseration. "We all have a woman in our past who makes us wish we'd decided to be monks, lad. Be thankful ye didn't have the misfortune to marry her."

Against his will, Declan chuckled and shook his head, as he looked at A.J., a man who was like an older brother. "Aye, then my folks would really have had reason to complain."

A.J. slapped him on his back and eased away, pausing as he was about to return to his captain's quarters. "Never regret your son. For too many are denied that dream."

Declan watched A.J.'s retreating back, listening as his footsteps faded away. Men's voices called out while playing cards, and Declan turned away from any temptation to join in. Without a brother by his side, he had no desire to be taken in by a card shark. Instead Declan considered A.J.'s words and attempted to find his courage to face his family.

CHAPTER 2

Fort Benton, Montana Territory, June 1867

A week later, the steamboat docked in Fort Benton on a hot, dry day in early June. Declan stood at the railing, searching for any sign of his brothers or father. However, no one had come to meet this boat, as it approached in the early evening hours. Whatever O'Rourke supplies that were on this boat would be set aside for retrieval tomorrow. Declan shook A.J.'s hand, ensuring he knew to visit him at the O'Rourke warehouse or home, and disembarked with Samantha and Gavin.

"Don't worry about our things," he murmured to her. "They'll be delivered." He held Gavin and motioned for her to follow him, as he made his way across the muddy Front Street, cut up by myriad wagon ruts. He only gave a passing glance at the thriving, boisterous, and burgeoning town and its businesses along the river. Instead he cut down a side street, away from the main thoroughfare that hugged the Missouri River.

"Home," he murmured, when he saw the large two-story house with a chicken coop in the back. An addition off the rear of the home ruined the precise symmetry of the house but afforded more space inside for the family. "We're a large family, Samantha," he murmured. "But they'll accept you." He saw the much younger woman shiver, before forcing a look of bored interest. "There's no need to be terrified."

Holding a slumbering Gavin to his chest, he approached the rear porch. Memories of racing inside after his brothers and up the stairs assailed him. Of sitting beside his youngest sister, Maggie, and chatting with her. Of watching his niece, Maura, play as she chased a chicken. How much had everyone changed in his absence? Would they truly want him back?

With a deep breath to ease his own doubts, Declan eased open the kitchen door just a hair, his gaze alert and his head cocked to one side, as he listened for the usual family chatter. When he heard the cacophony of conversation that heralded a typical O'Rourke family dinner, his hold on the bundle in his arms tightened, and he stood rocking in place. Familiar voices washed over him, as though a siren's call, urging him to take the last few steps and to finally be home.

Instead he closed his eyes, hearing his father's strong cheerful voice, as he called out loving words to his mum. A quieter voice responded that sounded like Mum, but Declan suspected was his sister Maggie, as it was youthful and not as heavily redolent of Ireland. Followed by his brothers' loud voices, as they joked and jabbed at each other. Laughter, always laughter and joy.

He took yet one more deep breath, kissing the bundle in his arms. How had he borne the years apart from them? Would they be eager to see him?

Gathering his courage, he forced himself to take the final steps into his parents' house. He pushed open the door, walked soundlessly, stilling, as he watched his family duck their heads for Da to say grace.

"May we always be fortunate enough to have plentiful work and food and a home to shelter us all. May we never forget the blessings of family and the joy of Mary's and Maggie's return. And may we see Declan returned to us sometime this year."

At the solemn rounds of "Amen," Declan watched his family dig into the meal in their controlled chaos, as an O'Rourke supper commenced. Battling tears, he swallowed to clear a thickness in his throat before he rasped, "I'm home, Da." His blue eyes shone with pain and relief, as he met his da's startled gaze.

"Declan!" Seamus yelled out, dropping his spoon and leaping up. He knocked his chair to the floor in his haste to reach his son, who'd been absent nearly two years. "Is it truly you? Have you come back to us?" He clasped Declan's shoulders in a bruising grip, as though afraid he were a ghost or that he would disappear again so soon after returning home.

Declan nodded, a tear leaking out of each eye as he met his father's incredulous stare. "Aye," he whispered. "I'm finally home."

"But you look nothin' like Declan," whispered Ardan, his eldest brother, as he gaped at him.

Declan shrugged, knowing he appeared much altered since the last time anyone in his family had seen him. Gone were the shaggy hair and the unkempt beard. Instead he had a genteel appearance about him, with a close-cropped haircut and a trimmed beard. His suit was finely styled and nothing like the backwoodsmen clothes he had favored. "'Tis me, Ardan."

When Seamus attempted to yank him into a bone-crushing hug, Declan took a step back and shook his head. "Nay, Da," he whispered, his eyes flashing with regret at the confusion and the pain in his da's gaze. At the perceived rejection of his father's joy at his return. "I can't have you crush him."

"What?" Seamus gripped Declan's shoulders and gave him a small shake. "You're not makin' any sense, Dec."

Unwrapping the blanket covering his chest, he revealed the baby cradled there. "My son, Da." His blue eyes gleamed with love and determination. "I have a son."

Seamus stared from the baby gazing up at him with alert curiosity to Declan and back at the baby again. "Sweet Jesus, to be so blessed," he breathed, his hand shaking, as it reached out to stroke the head of his grandson. "He's beautiful."

Declan smiled, devotion and love shining in his eyes as he beheld his son. "Aye, he is." When his father held out his arms, Declan transferred his precious bundle into his father's care. Glancing around the room, he saw everyone staring at him in absolute shock. "I'm home." He flushed at the inadequate words.

"Declan," his mum sobbed, as she pushed herself into his arms. "At last, you've returned to us." She pulled him down to hug him close. "You've been sorely missed, my lad. Home hasn't been the same without you."

He eased her away and flushed. "I doubt that, Mum, but thanks." He looked in the direction of his dumbfounded siblings, grunting as his youngest sister Maggie threw herself into his arms. "Maggie," he whispered.

"Oh, you're home at last. We're all together again." She swiped at her eyes, as she backed away and beamed at him, before smiling at her parents.

"Aye, just like we always should have been," Ardan said, as he pulled Declan close. "We've missed you something fierce, Dec." Soon all of Declan's siblings had abandoned their supper to gather around him to welcome him home.

Lorena Mortimer sat transfixed, as she stared at the man with the deep voice, cradling the bundle in his arms. Rather than appearing disgruntled or put upon, he stood with pride at the proclamation he had a son. As those around her rose to circle the newcomer, she peered between the men, women, and boys who had become her family to the man she would have recognized anywhere as an O'Rourke.

Although Lorena and her two sisters' arrival in Fort Benton a year ago had been inauspicious, the O'Rourke family had taken them in and had adopted them into their large loving family. Lorena looked at her glowing middle sister, Phoebe, who had married Eamon O'Rourke, and knew a large part of the sisters' acceptance had to do with Phoebe's marriage.

However, Lorena suspected the O'Rourkes would have been

generous in aiding the Mortimer sisters escape the clutches of their nefarious uncle, Uriah Chaffee, even without Phoebe's marriage to one of them.

Now finally Declan O'Rourke had returned, and the family was united again. Lorena tilted her head to one side, studying the man who was a few years older than her twenty-five years. Even though Eamon and Finn had often spoken of Declan as appearing like a wild backwoodsman, with long unkempt hair and a thick scraggly beard, now he appeared as polished and as urbane as her uncle. Declan's short ebony hair was cut irregularly, and she wondered if he took scissors to his own hair to prevent it from growing overly long. Where her uncle wore offensively bright suits, Declan's was a severe black, with a fine coating of dust.

She watched as he stepped farther into the room, a woman shadowing him. "Oh my," she breathed. Lorena cast a furtive glance in her sister Phoebe's direction to see if she had noticed the woman's appearance. Lorena saw Phoebe grip Eamon's arm, subtly nodding in the direction of the woman hovering in the doorway.

At her appearance, the cacophony of voices died down. Mary O'Rourke, the family's matriarch, approached the unknown woman with open arms and a friendly, if somewhat wary, smile. "Hello, dear," she murmured. "I'm certain this is overwhelming for you. Please come in and join us for supper."

Lorena watched with intense fascination as the O'Rourkes seamlessly accepted another person into their fold. For Lorena now understood: if this woman were important to Declan, they would accept her, rather than risk the loss of their beloved son. Lorena battled a bitterness that she had never known such love and understanding from her own mother and youngest sister, Winnifred. Pushing aside that rancor, she focused on the unfolding scene.

"Oh, I don't wish to be no bother," the young woman stammered out. "I ... I just need to stay near the baby." She was a tiny woman, who appeared to be not even five feet tall. Her lustrous black hair was pulled back in a braid, and her brown eyes shone with embarrassment, as though she were unaccustomed to being the center of attention.

Lorena watched as Mary and Seamus O'Rourke exchanged significant glances.

"Because you're the mother?" Mary asked in a confused voice, although Lorena could detect no censure in her tone.

"Mum, she's not Magnolia," Finn called out. "I don't know who she is, but she's not ..." He broke off when he saw the tormented expression on his older brother's face. "She's not her," he finished lamely, sharing an anguished look with his brother Eamon. Together, they had always been known as the O'Rourke twins because they were so similar in age, appearance, and actions. However, Eamon had married the previous year, and Finn had been slightly out of sorts since.

"No," Declan said, as he cleared his raspy throat. "This is Samantha. She's helping me with Gavin."

"Yes," Samantha said, flushing. She spoke in a voice barely above a whisper. "I'm the wet nurse."

Mary flushed but nodded. "We cannot thank you enough for traveling all this way and ensuring our grandson was well taken care of."

Flushing, Samantha ducked her head. "Oh, it was nothing, ma'am. I never thought to have such an adventure! Riding in a steamboat, attacked by Indians, to see such a wild, untamed land."

"Attacked?" asked Kevin O'Rourke, the second-eldest O'Rourke brother. "I presume none were harmed?"

Declan shook his head and smiled at Samantha, as she was eased onto the bench, where a full plate of food was set in front of her. "Eat," he murmured in his deep voice. "Keep up your strength for you and for Gavin."

Against her will, Lorena shivered at the quiet solicitude and concern in Declan's voice for Samantha. Although she detected no romantic interest between them, she nevertheless fought an envy at their easy camaraderie. At his quiet care of her. Lorena wished someone were as particularly interested in her well-being. With a frown, she forced away those thoughts and again focused on the O'Rourke homecoming.

"Gavin," Seamus breathed. "What a beautiful, proper name for the wee prince. You'll have so much fun playing with Cillian."

"Cillian?" Declan asked, his gaze never straying far from his son, now held by his mum.

"Niamh and Cormac's boy. Born in July last year," Mary said, as she kissed Gavin's head.

"Cormac?" Declan looked around at his family in confusion. "What about Connor?"

His da slapped a hand on his shoulder. "Oh, there's been a mighty number of changes since you've been away. And one of the most momentous is that Connor died, and Niamh married Cormac."

"And I married!" Eamon called out, unabashed joy in his voice.

"Married?" Declan asked, paling at the announcement. "I missed your wedding?" He gazed up and down the table, his gaze focusing on those he didn't know.

Lorena stilled as his sharp gaze homed in on her, as one of the newcomers at the table. Like most of his brothers and his father, Declan had piercing blue eyes. However, unlike his brothers, his gaze was filled with a penetrating sadness, as though he were in perpetual mourning. Her breath caught at the depth of emotions revealed. "I'm Lorena," she whispered through suddenly dry lips. "I'm a Mortimer sister."

"A Mortimer sister? What does that mean?" He stared in confusion at his brothers.

"It means, she's family," Eamon said. "Especially because I married Phoebe, her younger sister." Eamon tugged Phoebe over to introduce her to his brother.

Phoebe limped slightly, and Lorena noted how Phoebe flushed when Declan's gaze sharpened, as he noticed her infirmity.

Declan stared at Phoebe a long moment, so long in fact that Lorena was about to jump up to defend her sister. However, at the last moment, he beamed at her sister and murmured, "I can see how happy you make my brother. I wish I'd been here to welcome you to the family when you married. Please accept my congratulations now." He bent forward, kissing her cheek.

Focusing on his brother, Declan smiled, although the joy did not erase the underlying sorrow in his gaze. "You're happy, Eamon. I could wish for nothing more for my baby brother."

"Baby brother?" Eamon asked, as he launched himself forward for a bear hug. They slapped each other on the back twice. "Welcome home, Dec."

Lorena watched the scene with unabashed envy. Although she had been a part of the O'Rourke family for a year, she had never lost the sense that she was an interloper. Growing up with her sisters, she had never felt the close sense of camaraderie shown on a daily basis by the O'Rourkes. Rather than love, understanding, and humor, her mama's home had been filled with tension, disapproval, and disdain. Lorena had long ago learned that she would never truly belong.

As she stared at the reunion unfolding in front of her, she battled a deep yearning to have experienced such warmth and acceptance after her yearlong absence from her family some five years ago. Resentment bubbled up that she had never experienced such an unreservedly joyful homecoming. That hers had been shrouded in lies, silence, and shame. She let out a deep breath, wishing her life had been different. Gazing at Declan, she couldn't help but sense he would understand how she felt.

~

The following morning, Seamus wandered to the levee, his keen gaze searching for any sight of the captains he had come to know during the previous seasons. However, none were present among the recently arrived steamboats. "Lad, where's the captain to the *Deer Lodge*?" Seamus asked, as he gazed at the mounds of crates and other merchandise piled along the levee, waiting to be retrieved or to be delivered into the Territory.

The wiry man—a good five inches shorter than Seamus—turned to study him, as he puffed on his pipe. "*Lad*?" he asked, as he scratched at his thick brown hair. "I guess to an old-timer like you, I'm a lad."

Seamus stared at him, crossing his arms over his strong chest. "I'm not that old, lad."

The younger man chuckled. "And it's been a while since I've been considered a mere boy. I'm the captain, mister. Who's askin'?"

"You're the captain?" Seamus asked, his brows rising at the incredulous notion.

"Aye, I've been a river rat my whole life, although the lower Mississippi sure is an easier mistress to soothe. Not nearly as ornery as the Missouri." He puffed on his pipe, his brown eyes gleaming with curiosity and goodwill. "You have the look of Sonny about you. You his pa? The famous Mr. O'Rourke?"

Seamus flushed and ducked his head. "I'm not famous. And, if you're talkin' about my fine son Declan, aye, I'm his da. And proud of it."

Holding out his hand, the captain said, "I'm A. J. Pickens. Call me A.J. Only my crew calls me captain." He smiled with satisfaction after they shared a firm handshake. "And you are famous, O'Rourke. There's talk in the drawin' rooms of Saint Louis about you. And about other men who want to come up and try to steal away some of the monopoly you have. Money always makes a man jealous."

Seamus laughed. "And rash. 'Tis too often unpleasant to see what a man will do to earn a dollar."

A.J. nodded, his gaze solemn. "Aye. I've seen greed blind a man too often in my life."

Seamus looked at the crates waiting to be moved. "Don't be fooled, A.J. I don't have a monopoly. I was the only foolish one to strike out and to give it a go in '63 here in Fort Benton. Besides, I'm fortunate I have my family. I don't have to depend on partners or itinerant help to run the store." He smiled at A.J. "Call me Seamus."

"Well, Seamus, what do you think of your grandson?" A.J.'s brown eyes gleamed with challenge and concern.

Seamus appeared thunderstruck, as he stared at the younger man. "He's a beautiful lad. So bright and cheery."

"So you don't mind your boy showin' up unmarried, a bastard in tow?" A.J. asked with a lifted brow.

"Don't ever refer to anyone in my family that way again," Seamus growled. "No one in my family is unwanted. All are cherished and beloved." His cheeks flushed, and his eyes flashed with anger.

Smiling with satisfaction, A.J. bit on his pipe. "I told Sonny that he had no reason to worry. That the doubts and fears were his alone."

Seamus froze, his ire seeping from him as A.J.'s words penetrated his anger. "What?" he rasped. "Declan was worried we'd … we'd …"

"Reject him or his babe because he's unwed—an' the mother was a worthless woman, from the sounds of it." A.J. shrugged. "Your lad's carrying a season's worth of freight in guilt, Seamus. Thought you should know."

"Why tell me? You don't even know me," Seamus asked.

"Do you think folks don't talk?" The captain shrugged. "I'm a river rat, and one of the best commodities to barter is a good story. Always gets you a swig of decent whiskey or more tobacco for your pipe." He took another puff on his pipe. "You might think you live a quiet life in the backwaters in the middle of nowhere. But the story of the reunion of you and your wife is gainin' *infirmary*."

"*Infirmary?*" Seamus asked, scratching his temple. "Do you mean *infamy?*"

"Aye! You play along as well as your boy. Drives my dear Bessie mad, but then I think a little insanity goes a long way to helpin' keep a marriage interestin'." He winked at Seamus. "I never had to fight for my sweet Bessie the way they say you had to fight for your wife. We're parted more than we like, but we have months together, when I'm not on the river."

"Mary would hate that," Seamus murmured. "She doesn't want another night apart ever again."

A.J. beamed at him. "So it is true. Your story isn't a made-up fairy tale. I felt a fool, givin' away so much whiskey, as I listened to it more than once. But a good tale on a long river float is worth the cost."

"'Tis no fairy tale, lad," Seamus said, his cobalt-blue eyes glowing with a deep happiness. "And there are years I'd rather forget. But we're together again, and that's what counts."

"Aye, an' you're prosperous now. Seems you have it all, O'Rourke."

A.J. puffed on his pipe, his teeth flashing as he half smiled. "It also seems I carried up half a storefront full of merchandise for you."

Seamus chuckled. "Well, my lads and I'll be by to pick it up today. Come by the house soon for a home-cooked meal. I want you to meet my Mary. You'll earn your whiskey money back when you tell the tale of sitting at her table, dining with her." He winked at the younger man and left to rustle up his sons, whistling a jaunty tune.

CHAPTER 3

The following morning, Declan stood just inside the warehouse door, watching his brothers work. Kevin, Niall, and Lucien unloaded crates, as they joked and told stories, moving around with an easy precision, while they organized the goods that would be sold to eager miners in the nearby family store. Kevin was a few years older than Declan, with the look of their mum about him. The first O'Rourke brother to marry, he appeared more contented than ever with his choice in his Aileen.

Niall was Da's eldest son with his second wife, Colleen. The woman Da had married after he believed Mum had died. Declan shied away from thinking about Colleen, instead focusing on his younger brother who had transformed into a man in his absence. Gone were the slightly chubby cheeks and the gangly limbs. Instead Niall was long and lean, with the lithe grace of an O'Rourke. The only hallmark of his mother was his penetrating green eyes.

Declan's gaze flitted to the other brother helping Kevin. Young like Niall, at only seventeen, Lucien was strong and determined. He was the eldest of the two sons his mum had borne her French-Canadian husband, Francois Bergeron, after she had believed herself abandoned by Seamus in Montreal. Lucien looked the spitting image of Kevin, with auburn hair and hazel eyes, although he was taller, with broader shoulders. The one trait he had inherited from his trapper father, Declan mused.

As Lucien spoke, Declan no longer detected the subtle hint of the French accent he'd had when Lucien had joined the large O'Rourke family at their mother's return two years ago. Nor did he appear reticent about his place in their large family.

While Declan stood with his shoulder leaning against the doorjamb, he was struck with the fact that he no longer knew where his place was in his own family. Rubbing at his aching chest, Declan realized how much life had continued without him. Ardan now worked at the café with his wife. Kevin was married and successfully ran the warehouse with two other brothers. Eamon had married too, and Niamh had another child and a new husband. Looking around the warehouse, the one space that had always given him a sense of purpose as he helped put things to rights, Declan saw he had no place here. He was not needed.

His chest tightened as he fought panic. All he had thought would be certain had altered on him. Nothing was constant. "Except change," he murmured to himself, as he watched his brothers work with ease without him. "Was I even missed?" he whispered.

As a hand clapped his shoulder, he jerked, and he turned to stare at his father, who watched him with cautious hope. "You're stayin', lad?" Seamus asked in a low voice. "You're not runnin' away again an' leavin' me to mourn your absence?"

"Da?" Declan asked, as he shook his head. He waved around at the smooth operations of the warehouse. "I've not been missed."

"That's a bunch of malarkey, and you know it," Seamus said. "Every day you were missed. Every day we wished you home. Every day we prayed for your safe return." He paused as he gazed at his beloved son. "You're home again, and the family's complete. You've brought your son home to us too. Don't leave again."

Declan glanced into the warehouse, where he noted his brothers were no longer chattering away. "I've no plans to return to Saint Louis. For too long, my dreams have been of my life here, with our family." Taking a deep breath, he admitted, "But I need something to do."

"Ah, as to that, you could look at a few crates. The lads have been too busy to see to them yet. And you know we'll have more supplies arrivin' soon on another steamboat." Seamus winked at Declan, as he squeezed his shoulder and propelled him into the warehouse toward a corner of the large space. A mound of crates lay in a haphazard pile in a corner. "I believe they are all for a new project, but I might be wrong. Ensure they arrived without rot or water damage."

Declan stared at him in confusion, before moving to a crate and hefting it down to open it with a crowbar. After wrenching open the crate, he pulled off the lid and stared at the contents in confusion. "Books?" he whispered to himself. "Why would we order books?" He looked to his brothers, but they were busy putting away mining implements, and his da was nowhere in sight. Declan covered the crate, before moving to the small office to the side of the main room. "Da?" he asked. "Why books?"

Seamus smiled at him. "A business proposition was made last year, and I thought it worth exploring. A few crates of books seemed a small price to pay to see if it's profitable or not."

"But, Da …" Declan broke off at the squeal behind him, turning just in time to catch the woman throwing herself into his arms. "Niamh," he whispered.

"Declan!" she cried out, as she gripped him tight before pushing away. "You're home. You're finally back where you belong." She belted him on his shoulder and shook her head. "How could you stay away so long? How could you not know we'd be missin' you?"

Declan stared at her in wonder. Gone was the timid woman who attempted to live each day garnering the least amount of notice. Instead a vibrant, thriving woman stood before him with sparkling hazel eyes and shiny auburn hair tied back in a braid. "Niamh?"

She beamed at him, standing tall and with unabashed pride. "Aye, 'tis me. Much has changed since you departed."

Nodding, Declan said, "Da mentioned you married Cormac and have a son with him. A Cillian."

"Aye," Niamh said. "Cormac will be delighted you've returned, as will Dunmore. But they're both away just now." She shrugged. "'Tis the busy season, and they must work when they can." Niamh threw herself into his arms again, before spinning for the door. "I have to go. Mum an' Maggie are watching the wee beasts. Welcome home, Dec!"

Declan watched her race away as quickly as she had arrived. "'Tis truly Niamh?" he asked his da in wonder. "How could she have changed so much?" He sat down in the chair across from his father's desk, any concern about a crate of books forgotten after his sister's impromptu visit. Although he'd been away for nearly two years, now that he was here—sitting in his da's office, chatting over concerns with the man who he trusted most in the world—Declan felt like he had never been away. However, as he studied his da, he noticed subtle changes. More fine lines around his father's eyes and mouth. More gray hair peppered into the black. No matter how Declan liked to believe otherwise, time had continued, and life had gone on without him.

His da settled into his own chair, the wood creaking as he relaxed into it. After steepling his hands, he gazed with intense blue eyes at his son. "Niamh suffered while you were away," Seamus said, before shaking his head. "Nay, that's a lie. She's thrived while you've been away." He pinned Declan with a severe stare. "'Tis nothin' to do with your absence and everythin' to do with the death of Connor."

"Good riddance," Declan muttered.

"Aye, we, none of us, liked the man. But not one of us was wise enough to discover the true depth of his depravity. He beat her, Dec. And threatened Maura."

Declan paled, as he gaped at his father. "What?"

"Aye," Seamus said, staring at his son. "I've had over a year and a half to come to terms with my failings as a father, but I never will." He clenched and unclenched his fists resting on top of his desk. "I'd kill him ten times over for hurtin' my baby."

Declan rose and paced the small room. "How?" He sputtered to a stop. "Why?"

Seamus leaned forward and shook his head. "A man like that needs no reason." He sighed. "I'm just thankful Niamh trusted enough to marry Cormac. The man she always should have married."

Declan sat again with a *thud*. "How'd she ever trust again?"

Seamus tilted his head to one side, as though hearing a deeper question. "'Twasn't easy. An' Cormac had to show his patience and his love. But he did. And he's shown it every day since they married. He's not Connor."

Declan made a dismissive noise. "Nay, he never was. He was always a good man." With a sigh he rubbed at his head. "I hate to imagine what she suffered."

Groaning, Seamus leaned back in his chair. "Well, 'twas made worse by the arrival in town of a miserable man who claims he's a lawyer. I'm unconvinced as to the man's credentials, but I've yet to find proof I'm correct in my suspicions." He heaved out a breath. "A Uriah Chaffee arrived just after you left town. Missed the last ferry south and we've been stuck with him ever since. He's fascinated by the family, and I fear he has an alliance with Jacques Bergeron, but, again, I can't prove it."

"Jacques?" Declan asked, as he sat up and appeared ready to pounce. "Has he been seen lately?"

Shaking his head, Seamus stared out the side window a long moment. "No, and that's what worries me. Dunmore has tried to monitor his movement around the Territory, but the man disappeared last year." Seamus's jaw twitched as he clenched it, while thinking about the man who had terrorized Maggie and had threatened Henri and Lucien, Mary's two sons from her second marriage to Francois—from that time she had believed Seamus had abandoned her.

"Maggie's not alone now, Da," Declan declared.

"Aye, 'tis true. But Jacques is a trapper, an' this is a big Territory." He stared bleakly at his son. "And 'tis a reminder that, while we've attempted to protect Maggie, I failed Niamh." He shook his head, as the conversation ran full circle back to the eldest O'Rourke sister. "As for Uriah Chaffee, he's also the Mortimer sisters' uncle."

Declan shook his head in befuddlement, as though attempting to make sense of all the disparate connections. "The wayward lawyer, who may not be a lawyer, is related to the women who now live at the house? Is that why you gave them shelter?"

Seamus laughed. "Nay. We took them in because Eamon loves Phoebe. And she was nearly killed in her escape from the saloon. But 'tis a story for Eamon and his bride to tell you." He rose, winking at his son. "There's no need to hear every story in one sitting." He clapped Declan on the back and propelled him to the warehouse to continue his work on the crates filled with books. Only as he stared into the fifth crate did Declan realize his father had never answered his question about the large shipment of books from Saint Louis.

~

Lorena stood beside the small stream that led into the Missouri River. She had first come here with Maggie, and it had since become Lorena's thinking spot. Although she knew she shouldn't wander Fort Benton without a chaperone or an O'Rourke nearby because she never knew when her uncle would harass her, she had fallen into the habit of coming here alone. She found she needed a few moments during the week where she could be alone and think without listening to her youngest sister's bitter protestations about life.

She listened to the gentle birdsong, as swallows and finches flitted from branch to branch, before swooping overhead. She wished she were as free as those birds. That she had the courage to strike out and to demand what she wanted out of life. Instead she felt hemmed in by expectations. By fears. And by her own past failures.

The stream trickled over rocks, forming a soothing melody. Rather than stand on the creek bank, she moved to the shade of a bush, settling in for long moments of contemplation. The mossy smell of the creek was more enticing than any perfume she had ever smelled, calming her roiling thoughts.

Declan's return had set her on edge. Although Seamus had prayed every night for his son's return, she knew that the family had begun to fear that Declan would forever remain estranged. A part of her had hoped he would never return. She ducked her head in shame, as she admitted that thought to herself.

However, she had thought that on more than one occasion. The O'Rourkes were such a wonderful family. So accepting and loving of each other, and she resented that their lives were so seemingly blessed. As though they were under a magic spell, and all that bothered them or hurt them was easily healed. Happiness and joy were ever present, and she yearned for her share of that unending happiness and joy. Even Declan's return, with a baby out of wedlock, was seen as a reason to rejoice. Never did they make him feel shame or recrimination. Never disappointment.

Not even when the baby didn't look a thing like him.

She swiped at her cheeks as she laid back, staring at the bright blue sky with no visible clouds. She wished she had a bigger heart. That she were more generous, like the O'Rourkes. That she could love and love, knowing that that emotion would be reciprocated. Instead she knew she was miserly. That she only had so much love to bestow, and it had already been given away.

Declan walked back from visiting Ardan and Deirdre, anxious to check on Gavin. However, he knew that Gavin would be well looked after with his mum and sisters doting on him—and with Samantha diligent in her care. Declan smiled at the thought of his son smothered with love. For the O'Rourkes knew no other way to love than to love with every part of themselves.

He paused as he saw one of Phoebe's sisters walking from the direction of the stream toward the house. He scanned his memory, finally remembering she was Lorena. This morning she had left in a hasty, furtive manner after breakfast, and he was curious about what she did during the day. If she were a member of his family, he didn't want her to do anything that would harm those he loved.

He quickened his step and, just as quickly, froze when he saw a man stuffed in a black suit with a turquoise waistcoat step in front of her. By all appearances, this man's arrival was unwelcome, as the woman stepped away and jerked her head up in a haughty manner.

Declan decided to watch the interaction. However, when the older man gripped her arm, earning a squeal of pain, he rushed forward. "Sir, unhand her." He paused as the older man glared at him, as though he were the man evoking discomfort. "Now."

The older man released Miss Mortimer's arm, and Declan forced himself to focus on the older man, rather than Lorena massaging the reddened area on her forearm. "You owe her an apology."

"An apology? An apology?" The older man took a faux menacing step forward and jutted his belly out, bumping it into Declan, as though that were threatening to him. "You are the one interrupting a private conversation between me and my niece. You are the unwanted party in all this."

Shaking his head, Declan said, "I disagree. Any man who causes such distress to his niece is not worthy of being considered family." He reached out and ran his fingers over her damaged skin. "Are you well, Miss Mortimer?"

She shivered and shrugged. Finally she whispered, "As well as I can be, with him as my uncle."

"How dare you, you little hussy!" He swiped at his chin to clear it of spittle. "I am a respected lawyer. I am Uriah Chaffee. And I, not these infernal O'Rourkes, am the one who should be seeing to your future!"

Declan watched as any vivacity in her gaze faded to dull loathing.

"I will not work for Mr. Bell. I would rather consign myself to working at the Bordello."

"The Bordello," Declan gasped. "No fine lass would work there. Not when she has options." He stared from the uncle to the niece. "She's considered a part of my family, sir. You have no right to threaten her."

"Threaten her?" Chaffee rolled his eyes heavenward, as though speaking to Declan was more than he should have to bear. "I'm attempting to ensure she has decent employment, should I suffer an untimely death. I want to guarantee my nieces are well taken care of.

She's overdramatic, in the way of all women, in equating working as a saloon girl to working at the Bordello."

"Are you telling me that Phoebe wouldn't have been expected to entertain customers upstairs?" Lorena asked. "Or that you wouldn't expect the same of me?"

"Mere details," her uncle sputtered.

"It's not a mere detail to me, when I'm the one who'd have to do the so-called work," she spat out. Taking a deep breath, she said in a calmer voice, "You know better than to approach me. Why today?"

"I had hoped you had come to your senses. I can see I was mistaken!" Her uncle stormed away, muttering to himself about incalcitrant women.

Declan stood beside her a few long moments. "Shall I escort you home? Or is there somewhere else you'd rather go?"

"Home," she whispered. "Thank you."

After a few steps, he broke the tense silence. "Is he really your uncle?"

"I'm afraid so," she whispered. "And he's determined to have me or Winnie work for Mr. Bell. I think he owes Mr. Bell money."

Frowning, Declan said, "So you're to be used to pay off his debts?" At her nod, he growled his displeasure. "That's barbaric and cruel."

"Life is barbaric and cruel for most women. And rarely fair," she said, as she walked up the back steps to the O'Rourkes' kitchen. "Thank you for helping me. I would have escaped him, but it's always best for him to realize an O'Rourke is nearby."

Declan watched her slip inside his big family home, his mind filled with questions.

CHAPTER 4

That evening, at the knock at the front door, Lorena walked to answer it with a perturbed expression, flinging it open. "You know no one uses the front door," she snapped to the man standing there. "Everyone comes to the kitchen door." She pursed her lips, as she stared at the wiry gentleman with inquisitive brown eyes, whose gaze seemed to freeze her in place.

"I'll keep that in mind, missy," he said with a deferential smile that was mocking at the same time. "I was invited for supper by the man of the house himself. I'm hoping Mr. O'Rourke doesn't mind that I've accepted his invitation tonight."

Lorena flushed. "I beg your pardon," she stammered. "I … I'm not generally so … so …"

"Rude?" asked the man, as he hitched a finger through the suspenders covering his red-and-black-checkered flannel. "I ain't offended. My Bessie always takes offense at somethin' I say at some point durin' the day. Keeps things lively." He winked at her. "I'm A. J. Pickens. Call me A.J."

"I'm Miss Mortimer," she murmured, as she motioned for him to enter.

"Ah, a lovely woman like you must be promised to one of Seamus's

33

fine young sons." He watched her curiously, as she flushed as bright as a tomato. "Seems I'm mistaken. Well, you never know what will come about." He winked at her again, before following her through the living room to the kitchen.

"Mr. A.J. is here," Lorena said, as she entered, before scampering to her chair to observe rather than participate.

She watched as Seamus jumped up and clapped the man on his shoulder, as though he were a long-lost friend. After hearing the word "captain" bandied about, Lorena realized this was the captain who had manned the ship that brought Declan home—and a large supply of O'Rourke goods. She watched as Mr. A.J. charmed everyone present.

"I hope you like the meal I've prepared," Mary said.

"Oh, I ain't particular, missus," A.J. said, as he beamed at Mary. "I have to admit that I've been most desirous to make your acquaintance. The tale of your reunion with your husband is reaching epic status." He paused a moment. "Like that tale by that foreign man from many years ago that my Bessie goes on an' on about."

"Homer," Lorena murmured, flushing as everyone focused on her a moment.

"That's it. Homer. When I told my Bessie your tale, she sighed and said it reminded her of the *Audacity*, about that man comin' home and savin' his wife, after so many years away." He beamed at everyone, as he saw them biting their lips. "Did I say somethin' wrong?"

"I believe it's the *Odyssey*, sir," Lorena said.

"That's it! You're as smart as my Bessie," A.J. said, showing no embarrassment about misspeaking. "I find those big words a bother, and I rather like the ones I make up." He winked at Mary and Maggie, before sending another wink in Lorena's direction. "Find it keeps folks on their toes, as some can be mighty tense these days, now the War's over. You'd think they'd relax some." He shook his head and took an appreciative sniff. "*Whoowee*, sure smells like heaven in here. You're a lucky man, Seamus."

Seamus chuckled and propelled A.J. to a seat near his. "Aye, I am. We're fortunate we have food every day. But we're most fortunate that we're all together again, as we always should have been. A few of the lads are married, so they're not here every night. But we have a large family dinner at least once a week. And, for that, I'm grateful."

Lorena noted that Mr. A.J. sat in a chair that allowed him to face her, as he chatted with Seamus. Although he focused on the conversation with the eldest O'Rourke, and whatever he said made Seamus laugh frequently, the steamboat captain never ignored her.

After they had eaten supper, A.J. held out his hands for Gavin, murmuring, "There's my lad. I've missed you." He kissed the boy on his head and held him so Gavin could look out at the table, pounding his fists on the wood and playing with a spoon, as A.J. continued to speak with those around him.

"Missy, are you the schoolteacher in town?" he asked Lorena, as he pushed away his plate and all the silverware, except the spoon, so Gavin had room to play and yet to not cause any mischief.

"No, sir," Lorena said with a flush. "I help out where I'm needed. During the busy season, I wash dishes for Deirdre at the café."

"Wash dishes?" A.J. said, as he ran a hand down Gavin's back in an unconscious caress. "That don't sound like a good job for such an intelligent woman." He looked to Seamus. "No insult intended, O'Rourke, but you're wastin' her talents."

Seamus nodded, his eyes gleaming with mischief. "I know. We'll figure something out." He shook his head, indicating A.J. needed to drop the topic.

With a *humph* of disapproval, A.J. handed Gavin back to Declan. "Sonny's as smart too. Heard him goin' on an' on about topics that would bore any normal person, as he talked to his boy."

Declan laughed, as he held Gavin high for a moment, earning a squeal of delight from his son. "There's a lot of time to kill on a boat, A.J., and Gavin's a good listener."

"Aye, 'cause he won't talk back to ye," A.J. muttered with a shake of his head. Lorena noted him casting a furtive glance in her direction. However, his attention was diverted when Mary placed before him a bowl of rhubarb crumble with cream on top. "Oh my," he murmured, as he patted his stomach. "I said I'd make the one trip up the Misery,

35

but I might just brave a trip next year to see all of you again." He smiled at Mary and Maggie. "An' eat your fine food."

"If you like this, you'll be in heaven at what our Deirdre cooks," Mary said, as she rested her hand on Seamus's shoulder.

"It's not the Misery, sir. It's the Missouri," said Bryan, the youngest O'Rourke sibling at twelve, with a frown.

"Ha, that's what you think, boy!" A.J. said with a gleeful smile. "Indian attacks, sandbars that move from day to day, logs big enough to destroy a steamboat. Those ain't normal on a river this size. The Miss sure don't act like this." He shook his head, as the younger lads stared at him in wonder. He addressed Bryan. "Someday I'll have you be my cocaptain, an' you can see why it's the Misery."

"Did you hear that, Da?" Bryan exclaimed. "I'll be his cocaptain."

Seamus shrugged. "Aye, someday, lad. Someday." He shared a long look with A.J., who smiled with chagrin at filling one of the boys' minds with elusive goals. "'Tis better to dream than to live a resigned life."

"Aye," A.J. said, looking at Lorena. "Hear that, missy?" he called out. "Dream. Life's too short for resignation. Especially in a woman so young and pretty and smart."

Lorena ducked her head, blushing beet red this time, as she focused on the bowl of dessert in front of her. When the conversation continued around her, she sighed with relief. Glancing up, she saw Declan staring at her, and she met his intense gaze. For a brief moment, she wished she believed what Mr. A.J. said. However, she knew she deserved nothing more in her life. After her betrayal, she deserved nothing at all.

Lorena readied for bed that evening, praying she could slip beneath the sheets before Winnifred entered and found her awake. More often than not, Lorena acted as though she were asleep to ignore Winnifred's incessant prattle. Thankfully her sister's chatter faded away when she realized she didn't have an audience.

The door eased open, and Lorena swallowed a groan, while her youngest sister gave a chirp of satisfaction to find her awake. "Oh, finally!" Winnifred said, as she twirled into the room. "It seems you've fallen asleep earlier and earlier each evening. And I have the most delicious news to impart."

Lorena crawled under the sheet, her gaze filled with trepidation, as she knew her sister was never generous in her comments. "What would that be?"

Winnifred sat on her bed, slowly stroking a brush through her long, lush black hair. She sat so her curves were on their best display. Although Lorena found her sister's preening embarrassing, she knew Winnifred clung to every lesson their mama had taught them. "Uncle has found me the most wonderful man. Uncle believes he'll be a successful man in the Territory."

"Uncle?" Lorena asked, as she sat up, the sheet falling about her waist, and any attempt at playacting oncoming sleep was forgotten. "Why are you spending any time with that wretched man?"

Winnifred rolled her eyes at her eldest sister. "You are no fun anymore, Lo. Ever since the O'Rourkes took us in, you're far too serious. And since you made that devil's bargain with the eldest O'Rourke ..." She shuddered. "I'd hate to be so beholden to him."

"I'm not beholden to him. He's been very supportive and kind." Lorena bit her tongue, rather than say anything more, for she knew Winnifred would spread her words about town without thought to the harm she could do.

"*Supportive. Kind.*" She stared at her sister with a feigned guilelessness. "*Hmm*, it sounds as though you have another benefactor."

Flushing bright red, Lorena hissed, "I never had a benefactor. If you have one now, then you're a fool."

"Of course you had a benefactor. What else was Josiah?"

Lorena paled at the mention of Josiah. No one ever spoke his name. Not since he'd died, taking her heart and her hope with him. "You don't know what you say, Winnie. Let it be."

Winnifred gave a *humph* of disgust and threw herself onto her bed. "Why should I? Mama always said he was never good enough for you, and he wasn't. Stupid enough to join the War and get killed." She stared at the ceiling, muttering to herself.

Lorena froze, trapped in a maelstrom of memories. Her first kiss. The realization Josiah cared for her too. The fear and terror when she realized he'd leave her. The weeks of hoping he'd return. The letter. Always the letter. She let out a stuttering breath, digging her fingernails into her palms to force herself back to the present. "Leave well enough alone, Winnie," she rasped.

Propping herself up on one elbow, as she stared at her sister while laying on her side, Winnifred watched her with abject curiosity. "You know that Mr. Pickens sure was taken with you tonight. But it seems he has a wife." She gave a negligent shrug. "But you know most men aren't devoted to their wives, especially when they're so far away."

"How can you be so callous?" Lorena asked. Under her breath, she whispered, "How are you my sister?"

"I'm not callous," Winnifred protested. "I'm realistic. One of the Mortimer sisters needs to be. You're wasting your time, energy, and meager funds on an idiotic business venture. Phoebe's wasting her life as a wife. It seems I'm the one who must be the success in the family."

Staring at her youngest sister, Lorena frowned. She knew Winnifred would never imagine herself content with a traditional life, but Lorena suspected that was exactly what she needed. A husband who would prove his loyalty and his love, day in and day out. Just as Eamon had done for Phoebe. "I fear you're wrong," she murmured. "Only time will tell. And I hope that, by the time you figure out what you genuinely want, you haven't destroyed your true chance at happiness."

Lorena rolled onto her side, facing away from her sister, her last words rolling around in her head. For too long, she had believed those words about herself. That she had already ruined her one true chance at happiness. As the house settled and sleep beckoned, she allowed herself to wonder if that was true. Of if she'd allowed fear to dictate her dreams.

∿

S eamus rested in bed, his gaze never wavering from the door, as he awaited his beloved Mary's arrival. Although she had seemed delighted by their surprise guest this evening, he knew A.J.'s presence had meant more work for her and Maggie. When the door creaked open, he gave a sigh of relief. "Ah, love, you're finally here," he murmured.

She flashed a delighted smile, as she shut the door behind her and began her nightly ritual of preparing for bed. Seamus never tired of watching her taking down her hair or slipping her earbobs free of her ears. "Come," he murmured, holding out his hand for the brush. "Let me care for you, after you were so gracious to our guest."

She sighed with pleasure, as she sat on the bed with him kneeling behind her, his strong, nimble hands working through her hair. "'Twas no fuss, Shay." She winked at him. "Besides, the younger lads helped with cleanup. Bryan will give you a run for your money with the stories he will tell." She returned to the topic of their guest. "A.J.'s a delightful man. 'Twill be a sorry day when he sails away."

Seamus kissed the side of her neck, smiling when she gave another sigh of pleasure. "Aye, 'twill. He claims he's only to man a steamboat the one time to Fort Benton. I'm to use the time he's docked here to convince him to return next year. From what little Declan's told me, he's a fine captain. I believe he'll be a good friend."

"Do you think he sees more than the rest of us?" she asked, as she bowed her head forward when he began to massage and knead the muscles of her neck and shoulders. "He took a keen interest in Declan and Lorena."

Seamus stilled his ministrations a moment and then gave a grunt. "'Twould make sense, love, but can you see either of them trusting in love again?"

Mary's shoulders sagged. "No," she whispered mournfully. "I hate we weren't there for Declan, Shay. That he had to suffer alone."

"Aye," Seamus said. "But he's a man now, love. And we must allow him to handle this. He'll find his way through this too." He kissed her again, before speaking in a hesitant voice. "Do you ... do you adore wee Gavin?"

She spun to face him, her auburn and gray hair tumbling over one shoulder, as her hazel eyes flashed with confusion. "Adore him? Nay." She cupped her husband's cheek. "I love him. He's my grandson." She waited a moment. "All that matters is Declan's claimed him, Shay."

Seamus tugged her into his arms, rocking her from side to side. "Aye, *a ghrá*, that's all that matters. Thank you, my love, for always having the most generous heart."

~

"Da," Declan said, as he entered his father's warehouse office. "Do you have a moment?" He knew that was a rhetorical question, as his da would always make time for any of his children, no matter what task he was doing. Declan smiled. Unless Da was with Mum. Then his da would tell them to wait their turn.

"Aye, of course, Declan. We haven't had a chance to visit enough since your return." Seamus set aside a mound of papers in front of him and focused on his son.

Although only a few years had passed, Declan was still surprised to find more gray in his da's hair. More set-in wrinkles, especially around his eyes and mouth. However, the clarity and intelligence in his gaze had not diminished.

"What's bothering you, lad?"

Declan flushed and then shrugged. There had been little he couldn't discuss with his da. "I worry Lorena Mortimer is playing us false." He frowned when Seamus burst out laughing.

"Oh, Declan, how I've missed you," Seamus said, as he marshaled control. "You should worry about Winnifred, not Lorena." He nodded when he saw Declan staring at him in confusion. "Aye, Winnifred's been absent from supper of late. She's the Mortimer sister who'll bring trouble to the O'Rourkes. And, I fear, to Finn."

"Finn?" Declan breathed. "He's too sensible to ... to ..."

"To fall in love?" Seamus asked softly. "Nay, he's not. And nor are you." He paused as he waited for Declan to speak. When his son remained quiet, Seamus murmured, "You're too young to be so cynical. And far too young to believe you'll never love again."

"I didn't love," he said in a bitter tone. "I was played like the finest fiddle. I was a fool, an' I paid the price."

Seamus stared at him a long moment, an assessing glance that had always made Declan squirm in the past. This time Declan sat still, meeting his da's stare. "Is raising another man's child your penance?"

Heaving out a breath, Declan's shoulders stooped, as he lowered his head down to balance on the desktop. "How did you know?"

"From what Finn and Eamon told me, if he were your son, he should be a mite smaller. He shouldn't be nearly Cillian's size." He paused. "And he looks nothin' like an O'Rourke. Or like Mary's people."

Declan raised his head, his eyes gleaming with fierce loyalty and love. "He's mine, Da. Whoever his parents are, he's mine."

Seamus remained silent a long moment, staring into his son's eyes. Finally he smiled. "Aye, an' I'm glad of it. He's a fine lad, and I'm proud to call him my grandson."

Declan gaped at him, before covering his eyes. "I never thought you'd truly accept him. Or me again."

Seamus growled with displeasure. "When have I ever given you reason to doubt?" His eyes glowed with hurt. "You dishonor me, your mum, and your entire family with that comment." When Declan refused to look up at him, Seamus reached forward and clasped Declan's forearm. "I understand heartache. I understand despair. I understand hopelessness." He swallowed as he looked into his beloved son's gaze and saw all he'd described, along with unbearable weariness. "But I also know nothing is permanent. You will find a way to discover joy again. Laughter and happiness again."

"How, Da?" He took a deep breath and shook his head. "I wanted to return, triumphant. With a bride and a babe. Instead I return with a wet nurse and a babe who's not even mine." He snorted out a scoffing laugh. "Where's the accomplishment in that?"

Seamus's grip on his arm tightened. "You returned, Declan. *You* returned. That's what matters. You had enough faith in us to come home. To share your son with us, for, no matter what your head says, your heart knows he's yours."

Declan nodded, ignoring the single tear that coursed down his cheek. "Aye, he's mine. And heaven help anyone who says differently."

Seamus gave a grunt of approval, patting Declan's arm. "You'll find love but this time with a worthy woman. With all your brothers around, they won't allow you to fall for the wiles of another heartless lass."

Shaking his head, Declan murmured, "Finn and Eamon couldn't stop me. They tried, Da. But I wouldn't listen."

"Nay, they didn't have the courage and the mettle they have now. Eamon's a married man, and he's had to face losing the woman he loves. He'd fight you much harder this time." Seamus smiled. "But now you'll also have Ardan, Kevin. And me." He stared into his son's desolate gaze. "Give yourself time, lad." He paused. "Forgive yourself, and then you'll find a way to begin again."

Declan nodded, as another tear trickled down his cheek.

CHAPTER 5

A few days later, Declan grabbed a piece of toast and his mug of tea, ducking out of the house, as he ignored the curious stares and questions. He followed Lorena as she walked with a purposeful stride. He noted she paid no attention to the interested looks from men who had wandered away from the main street in town by the levee, called Front Street, her gaze always straight ahead. Declan imagined she'd never deign to smile, for he'd only ever seen her smile with her sister Phoebe, his sister Maggie, or with the incorrigible Mr. Pickens.

Rather than turn toward Front Street, she veered farther away from the bustling riverfront area. "Where are you going?" he muttered to himself. He paused when she stopped in front of a building that looked like an old restored cabin.

She extracted a key, unlocked the door, and pushed it open. Rather than slamming it shut, she left it wide open.

His curiosity fully piqued, he wandered to the cabin, walking silently on the small wooden front step. He poked his head in, jumping back as she screamed in fright. "I'm sorry, miss. I never meant to scare you."

She stared at him with frank skepticism. "Perhaps not but you're a horrible spy. I knew you were following me the entire way here." She held a hand to her chest. "I thought you'd see that I arrived safely and would leave. I never expected you to follow me in here."

"How'd you know I was followin' you?" he sputtered. "And what is this place?" He stared around in confusion, setting down his mug on a crate.

"I knew," she said, as she grunted to push him out of the way to hang up her Open sign in bright letters, "because so few men approached me. Or called out impudent comments."

Declan scowled. "That isn't right, miss. You should be able to walk through town without every man leering at you."

Rolling her eyes at him, she brushed past him again. "I have a feeling you eyed every attractive woman who came to town too." When he flushed, she nodded, as though having proven her point. "The only thing I have protecting me is that most men understand they would have to answer to Seamus O'Rourke and his sons were they to harm me. And few are willing to risk his or their wrath."

Frowning, Declan leaned against the doorjamb. "That's all you have protecting you? The threat of violence from my father and brothers?" He considered what she'd said as he ate the piece of toast in a few quick bites. "From me?" At her nod, he swiped his hands clean and frowned at her. "That seems rather feeble."

"Perhaps, but it's better than what I had when I disembarked here a year ago." She grunted as she lifted a heavy box, panting as she set it on a table.

Declan looked around the small one-room space and frowned. He had thought she was escaping his parents' house to have illicit meetings with a lover. Instead this was a room filled with boxes and crates with not even a chair in sight. "What is this place?"

"Well, it's not much right now, but it will be Fort Benton's first bookstore," she said, a proud gleam in her eye and with a quirk of her lips.

Declan waited, hoping she would fully smile. However, she sobered at his silence and spun away to attack a box. "A bookstore. Don't you need shelves and books?"

She kicked a crate. "I have books. And the crates will be the shelves. For now."

When she bent to pick up another box, he rushed forward, gently pushing her aside to lift the heavy box. "You shouldn't be lifting such heavy boxes. You'll harm yourself," he admonished. "Come. I'll stay here until you have this set up to your satisfaction. Consider me your beast of burden."

Lorena flushed and shook her head. "I could never ask you to be here with me, when you have important work at the warehouse."

Shrugging, Declan pried open the nearest box and began lifting out titles. "How are we to arrange them?" He glanced over his shoulder, meeting her apprehensive gaze. "I'm not needed there anymore. My younger brothers have taken my place." He turned away, hiding any bitterness or remorse. "As they should have. I've been away too long."

"They missed you every day," she whispered. "Prayed for you."

He nodded, his vision blurry, as he stared blindly into the box. "As I did them," he murmured. "But I couldn't return any sooner. I had to ensure my son, … my son was safe." He spun, a bright smile pasted on his face. "Now put me to work, Lorena. There's quite a bit to be done."

Hours later, boxes and crates were strewn around the store, and a system for organizing the books had yet to be decided upon. "I don't see why we don't just arrange them by type of book. You know? Books women like. Books men like. Bible books." He shrugged.

Lorena giggled. "*Bible books?*"

He smiled, his gaze lit with happiness as he saw her unfettered joy to be surrounded by so many tomes. "Do you know how many books I've unpacked that have to do with sermons? Whoever packed these crates must have thought we were a very pious group."

"Or severely lacking in piety," she said with another giggle. "If they only knew we had a traveling priest, and he preferred the cities of

Virginia City and Helena." She shrugged. "Not that we need a priest that often."

"Were Eamon and your sister married by a priest?" he asked, unable to hide his concern.

"Of course, and your father tried to convince the man to remain here year-round. Said he'd build him a proper church with a small house nearby. But the pious man said this wasn't the place of his true calling." She shrugged, as Declan laughed.

"Sounds like Da. He'd like us all to go to Mass each week. But he understands we can't." He smiled at her. "So what do you think of my idea? 'Tis sound, is it not?"

She stared at him a long moment. "The more time you spend with your family, the more you sound like them again. It's as though you lost Ireland while you were away from them."

He flushed and shook his head. "I lost more than that, lass." He turned away, his hands on his lean hips. "Now what about the five-and-dime novels over here? And the others over there?" He pointed to the wall on the other side. "Do you want customers to be able to look around and to find what they want? Or are you afraid they'll steal copies?"

"*Steal?*" she asked, with a furrowed brow. "I'd like to think my customers are honest."

Declan gave her an incredulous look. "You've been in this town a year. Surely you know better." He paused, swiping at his forehead. "While you think about it, I'll open the other windows. We need more air." He moved to the windows on the side and at the rear of the building, frowning, as they were stuck and wouldn't open. "What's wrong with your windows?" he asked, as he grunted and pushed with all his might.

"They stick. Some days they open. Some days they don't." She shrugged. "I don't have the money to replace them."

He glared at them. "Aye, and 'tis doubtful spare windows came on a shipment up from Saint Louis." After another attempt to open one, he gave up. "Better than breakin' the bloody thing."

She laughed and shook her head. "You're not responsible for

anything that happens here, Declan. This is my establishment. It will succeed or fail due to what I do. Or don't do."

He pulled over an upended crate and sat on it. "What made you think about peddlin' books?" He smiled at her as she sobered. "Da's willin' to peddle almost anythin' if it'll bring a profit. I'm certain he'll back you."

Flushing, Lorena admitted, "Your father *is* helping me. I could never do this on my own. He has faith in what I want to create." When Declan sat with quiet patience to hear what that was, she said, "A successful store, where those who love books can congregate. Where men and women can trade in their books for another one, before they journey farther into the Territory. And a place for residents to meet in the winter that isn't a saloon or the café." She flushed.

Declan smiled. "Sounds lovely, but how will you make it work? Are you lending or selling the books?"

Lorena appeared deep in thought for a moment. "I'm going to sell the books. If the book is new, like most of the books I have here now, they will be more expensive. However, if a patron wishes to sell me a book, I will purchase it at a reduced price, give the patron a store credit toward more books, and resell it at a higher price to a new patron. I know that I won't be able to order new books every year and that there will be times when I have more demand than books."

Declan tilted his head to the side, as he thought through her plan. "So 'tis like a lending library in a way, although you'll always end up the winner."

Laughing, Lorena nodded. "Yes, in theory. However, I've found little rarely works out as I imagined."

"What's the name of your store?" He raised his hands, sweeping wider, as though to indicate a grand name in bold lettering.

Ducking her head, she said, "I don't have one. Not yet." When he gaped at her, she moved around the space, shuffling books from crate to crate. "I never thought this would be more than a dream. Even when Mr. O'Rourke said he would order the books, I never thought they'd arrive. That the steamboat would catch fire. Or that the crates would fall overboard. Or ..."

Declan laughed, his worries seemingly far away, as he looked much younger and less serious. His blue eyes sparkled with mischief. "You've spent too much time reading those books of yours. You've an imagination to match." He leaned forward as he rested on the crate and made a face, as though he were deep in thought. "How about Lorena's Library?"

Immediately shaking her head, Lorena flushed. "No, no, I can't have it named that. I ... It isn't just mine. Your father invested. It's part O'Rourke."

He lifted a shoulder. "Well, we can't have another O'Rourke name on a building. People would start to think there's a conspiracy. And your name's pretty." He winked at her, crossing his strong arms over his chest, wrinkling his waistcoat. "How about A Reader's Paradise?"

She wrinkled her nose. "Seems a bit presumptuous, doesn't it?"

"If it's not presumptuous, it won't be successful. You must have believed someone would want to purchase your books, or you never would have started this store." He stared at her, fascinated, as he watched her fidget under his close perusal. "Your store won't prosper if you don't believe in it. For, if you don't, why should anyone else?"

"That's not fair," she whispered, her beautiful green eyes filled with hurt.

"Perhaps not," he said, as he rose, "but the truth rarely is. Take a leap of faith. Open A Reader's Paradise, and watch your customers flock to your store. I dare you."

Declan returned home after being shooed away by Lorena. He fought feeling disgruntled that she wanted time without him in her own store, but he knew she had earned that right. And he knew she would be safe there, as Maggie had stopped in to help.

He slipped into his parents' house, eagerly listening for any sign of his son. He'd had too little time with him lately, although Gavin had been thoroughly spoiled with the love lavished on him from his aunts, uncles, and grandparents. Declan froze in place upon entering the living room at the sight of his da, walking a slow circuit around the room, Gavin in his arms, as he chatted to the boy. Gavin's cheeks were drying from a recent crying spell, and he seemed mesmerized by Seamus's voice.

"So you see, my dearest lad, you have to know when the land is fertile and to plant at the perfect time to ensure your crop will receive all the sunshine and water it needs to thrive. Thataway you'll have enough to feed your family and to sell at market." He kissed little Gavin's cheek, swiping away his tears. "Now, my little love, I won't be seein' the green shores of Ireland again, but you or your sons might. And I can teach you all I know, so they'll know what to do." He sighed, as he rocked in place, his eyes closed. "I don't have any experience farmin' here in this barren land, but we've enough businesses to keep you occupied. And I suspect your da will find his own way."

Declan cleared his throat, unable to smile, nearly overcome with emotions as he stared at his father, talking to his son. When Gavin reached out for Declan, he held out his arms, cradling his son to his chest. "There's a love," he murmured, kissing Gavin's head. "Da?" he murmured. "You still dream of farming? Even after all these years?"

Seamus ducked his head and appeared chagrined. "Well, there's no shame to have more than one love when it comes to work. For all work is admirable, if it brings food, shelter, and security to your family."

Declan nodded, although he appeared worried. "Aye, but it sounds as though you miss it."

"I felt alive diggin' in the dirt," Seamus said with an abashed grin. "An' there's no shame in admittin' that." He paused as he looked at his son. "What is it, lad?"

"You believe he'll return someday? To Ireland?"

Nodding, Seamus ran a hand down his grandson's back. "Aye, one of my offspring will. I'm certain of it."

"You miss it," Declan whispered.

"Always. Every day." Seamus cleared his throat and blinked a few times to diminish any semblance of tears. "Although the yearnin' for home has decreased with the return of your mum." He smiled. "I find her presence soothes most aches in my soul."

Declan unconsciously mimicked his da's previous motion, rocking in place with Gavin in his arms, to the point Gavin heaved out a breath and tumbled into sleep, his head butting into Declan's chin. Grunting, Declan shifted his son, so his head rested on his shoulder. "I'll forever wish I'd made a more sensible choice."

"Did you never think that you did?" Seamus asked, as he studied his son, rocking too, although he wasn't holding a child. "Did you never consider you'd found a woman who would help teach you the lesson you needed to learn at the time you needed to learn it?"

Declan closed his eyes, holding his son close. "'Tis hard to admit I was such a fool that I was in need of such a terrible lesson."

Seamus sighed, gripping his son's shoulder. "Ah, lad, that's when you know you're most in need of it. I give thanks, every day, that you've returned and that you brought Gavin with you. That you were not denied the joys of raisin' your beautiful boy."

Suddenly fighting a deep emotion, Declan whispered, "How do you do it? How do you remain so filled with hope and joy?" He sniffled. "How do you rejoice, when all I feel is an unrelenting despair?"

Seamus gripped both shoulders, as though he could take his son and grandson into his arms and shelter them from all harm. From all of life's pain. "Never will I lose hope. If the past few years have taught me anythin', 'tis that I should hope and always keep faith."

Declan sighed into Gavin's light-brown hair, ruffling it with his deep exhalation.

"One day, you'll forgive yourself. And you'll come to realize 'tis all right to love another." He smiled, as his son gaped at him incredulously.

"I'll never love again," Declan proclaimed.

"Ah, lad, *never*'s a long time for a man with such a big heart." Seamus squeezed his shoulders again and slipped from the room, leaving Declan deep in thought.

～

Lorena looked up from her book to find a large shadow in the doorway. Although she admonished herself for her instinctual fear, her breath caught, and she waited to see what the stranger would do. When Declan O'Rourke entered, she let out her pent-up breath and flushed with embarrassment. "You didn't have to scare me into a witless ninny," she snapped.

"I scared you?" he asked, as he raised an eyebrow. "A man standing on your library's doorstep frightened you?" He shook his head, as he scratched at his neck. "I worry you won't have much success if you can't even chat with the customers because you've fainted away in fear at their mere presence."

"Stop mocking me," she hissed, her eyes flashing with anger.

"I'm not. I'm concerned for Da's investment."

She slammed down her book. "Of course that's all that would concern you. Money. Profit. You never realize there's more to life than finding a way to earn more and more and more."

His blue eyes gleamed with warning as he stared at her. "Don't presume to judge me when you barely know me."

"Take your own advice."

Declan sighed and nodded. He ran his hand through his hair, grimacing when he sent the short locks on end. "Aye, I'm sorry, lass. I'm bein' an ass because I'm upset."

Letting out a long breath, Lorena studied him. "You seemed surprised when you ran your hand through your hair," she murmured.

He chuckled mirthlessly. "Aye." He ran his hand through the short strands again. "I'm always surprised to find my long hair gone. 'Tis as though I lost a part of me when I cut my hair."

"Then why'd you do it?" she asked, flushing as his penetrating gaze homed in on her again.

"You already know the answer, if you care to consider it." When she remained quiet, he sighed. "I wanted to fit in. I was tired of being a curiosity among people who I wanted to emulate. Too late I realized they weren't worthy of my esteem." He turned away—but not before she saw his chagrin at having revealed too much.

"It's hard not to give in to the demands of others. Or to delude ourselves into believing giving away small pieces of ourselves will not lead to any lasting pain." She smiled bravely as she met his startled look, when he faced her again. "I know what it is to want to fit in. To not be considered an oddity. But I've discovered the price can be too high."

"What happened to you?" he asked. "Why do you hide on the margins of life, observing everyone but rarely participating?" He paused before another question burst out. "Why does the shadow of a man frighten you?"

She shook her head. "I don't know you, Mr. O'Rourke." She tilted her chin up, as she faced the disappointment in his gaze.

"No, and I fear you'll never allow me to," he murmured. "Do your own sisters know you?" At her jerk, as though his question had inflicted bodily harm, he swore under his breath. "I beg your pardon."

"I don't understand why you believe you have the right to ask me such questions. It isn't as though you're on good terms with your family members. Eamon and Finn are still hurting after you forced them away a year ago. Have you ever spoken with them?"

Declan smiled, a grudging admiration in his gaze. "No, I haven't. But I will." His smile broadened. "Like I thought, you're a keen observer." He sighed, as he looked around the now tidy space. "As for me, you're stuck with me and my presence. Da's worried some of the townsmen and transients are becoming a bit too forward in their treatment of you. Thus I'm to sit here each day, be your Ezra."

"Ezra?" she stammered. "I don't know what you mean."

"Ezra's the man who watches the door and guards the Sirens. The women at the Bordello." He flushed. "I admit, bad example. I'm to be your watchdog. Ensure none of the men get out of hand."

She stomped her foot on the ground and glared at him. "You'll scare away all my customers as you sit there and glare at them!"

"If they're truly interested in books, rather than gawkin' at you, then they won't be intimidated by my presence. Besides, it's Da's wish."

She let out an aggrieved huff, for she knew what Seamus O'Rourke wanted was as good as gospel. Although she would never admit it to Declan, she was silently relieved he would be here. A few of the men who had perused the books the previous day had been a bit too friendly. "Fine. You can stay. But you must be silent."

"You'll never know I'm here."

"So I fervently hope."

CHAPTER 6

A few mornings later, Lorena stood on her sister's porch and took a deep breath. Although near the large O'Rourke family home, it was separate enough that Phoebe and Eamon had their own space. They were able to join in on any of the O'Rourke events that they wanted but could build their own life as a married couple, with the support and love of the extended family. Every day Lorena waited for the news that Phoebe was with child. And every day that she was spared such an announcement, she gave thanks. She feared envy would eat her alive.

Taking another deep breath, she knocked on her sister's door. Lorena had an hour before she needed to open her store, and she hadn't spent enough time with her middle sister lately. As the door eased open, her smile faded. "Phoebe? Are you ill?"

Phoebe grimaced, patting at her long blond hair tangled around her shoulders. "No. Not in the way you mean."

Paling, Lorena whispered, "You're in a family way." When Phoebe nodded, staring at her with wide terrified eyes, Lorena swallowed her unwanted emotions, pulling her sister into her arms. "You'll be the most wonderful mama, Phoebe."

"How do you know that?" Phoebe cried out, as she clung to her eldest sister. "What if I'm like Mama? What if all I see is fault and something to ridicule?" She pushed away from her sister, swiping at the tears coursing down her cheeks. "What if I look at my baby and wish it were other than it is?"

Lorena fought tears as she saw her sister's torment. Cupping Phoebe's face, she whispered, "You'd never do that. You'd never treat a child created out of love with anything other than devotion. You'll only ever look at your child as the benediction it is. Trust me, Phoebe." She pulled Phoebe close, as her sister cried on her shoulder.

"I'm so afraid. And no O'Rourke will ever understand. All they do is love and love and love."

Lorena made a soothing noise. "Of course they'll understand, Phoebe. You've heard about their miserable stepmother. And Maggie's horrible stepfather. They know what it is to have someone in their life who's cruel and incapable of caring for them." She kissed her sister's head. "Trust Eamon. He'll understand."

Biting her lip, Phoebe stared at her sister, her tear-dampened cheeks ignored. "He stares at me as though he's memorizing the hours he has with me. I think he's afraid I'm ailing."

Lorena groaned. "Tell him so he's not afraid. Let him revel in his good fortune with you. For having a child with a man who adores you as he does is something to celebrate."

Phoebe smiled at her sister and moved to the stove to set on the kettle. "Will you stay for a cup of tea?" At her sister's nod, she set out cups and prepared the pot. "What brought you by? Are you well?"

"Of course I'm well. I'm always well." She sighed. "Although I'm annoyed beyond comprehension."

"Why?" Phoebe asked, as she found a hand towel to swipe at her face. She sat, combing her hair, before pulling it back in a loose knot.

Lorena wandered the small living space, tidying it up for her sister. She flung the quilt over the bed, smoothed down the tablecloth on the small dining table for two, and then moved to the sink to do the small pile of dishes. As she scrubbed away, she said, "Declan's driving me insane."

"Declan?" Phoebe asked, as she sat with a *thud* on a chair, smiling appreciatively at her sister who helped clean her house. "Why? He's morose and barely speaks to anyone. Eamon's losing hope he'll ever reconcile with his brother."

"Oh, he speaks. He chatters incessantly." Lorena dunked a dish in the pail of clean water, then set it aside. "He has an imagination like I never knew was possible, Phoebe. And he's curious. About everything. Although he claims he should be a backwoodsman, with the hair and clothes to match, I think he should be a professor."

"A teacher," Phoebe breathed.

"Yes, exactly. He should share his curiosity and joy for learning with others." She shrugged, as though what she said didn't really matter. "Although he'd never take what I had to say seriously."

Phoebe watched her oldest sister work, grimacing as she slammed down dishes with such force she feared she'd crack them. Lorena had always been the most controlled, the demurest of the Mortimer sisters. It was as though she attempted to distract anyone from her red hair—to prove that she was not hotheaded or heedless of consequences. As she studied her sister, Phoebe realized this was the most animated she'd seen her sister in years.

"He promised he'd be a *silent* sentry," Lorena muttered.

"If he had been, I doubt you'd have realized how intelligent he was. Or that you're attracted to him." Phoebe's eyes shone with mischief, as her sister squealed and spun to face her.

"Attracted to him? Are you insane? Of course I'm not attracted to him." She closed her eyes, as though praying for patience. "He's a good-looking man. All O'Rourkes are. But that doesn't mean ... doesn't mean ..." She stammered to a stop, before she rubbed at her forehead. "I can't like him, Phoebe."

Any teasing faded when Phoebe rose to approach Lorena, as though she were an injured wild animal. "Why, Lo? You like him. He likes you. I know there's so much I don't understand. But, if the two of you understand, that's what matters. Isn't it?"

"I've done things, ... things that are unforgiveable." Lorena ducked her head. "And I couldn't live with his or your or anyone's disgust."

Phoebe pulled her close, rocking her side to side. "Stop it, Lo. Stop it right now. Nothing you could have done would disgust me. Would make me stop loving you like the beloved sister you are." She cupped Lorena's face, her gaze earnest and wise. "I know what it was like growing up with Mama. I know the expectations she had. And I know we all did what we could to keep her happy. You should feel no shame because you survived our childhood. You should feel shame if you don't give thanks, every night, that we have a chance for a different life now."

A tear trickled down Lorena's cheek. "Oh, I do give thanks, Phoebe. I do. But I fear too much happened during my time away. I fear I'll never overcome it."

Phoebe smiled. "You're strong, Lo. Stronger than any of us. I know you will."

～

Lorena returned to her bookshop, staring into space. Closing her eyes, she attempted to bury images from the past. Memories that had the potential to overwhelm her. She took a deep breath and then another, as she focused on the town noise in an attempt to ground herself.

"If you go about life daydreaming, girl, you won't have any success," a snide voice called out.

Lorena's eyes blinked open, and she stared at Aileen's aunt, Mrs. Davies, who stood inside her store, sneering at her displays of books.

"Or you'll be robbed blind, as men sneak in and steal your merchandise. It only proves a woman should never be left in charge of an enterprise." Janet Davies sashayed into the bookstore, her heels clicking on the wood, as her skirts swirled around her ankles. Rather than the pristine dresses she had worn upon her arrival to Fort Benton some two years ago, this formerly navy-blue dress was faded to a near gray. However, Janet Davies held herself and walked as though she were the master of all she surveyed.

Lorena stood tall, her gaze inquisitive, as she studied the woman rumored to be her uncle's paramour. Or one of them. "There are plenty of women who run successful businesses."

Scoffing, she shook her head. "Ha! You've had your head filled with mush as much as any O'Rourke. Now you'll try to convince me what the Madam does is honorable and a decent way for a woman to earn a wage."

Unable to hide a sly smile, Lorena bit her lip before murmuring, "Well, it seems as honorable a living as a man's mistress in order to maintain one's lifestyle." Her green gaze met and held Mrs. Davies' gaze, now glowering, for Lorena's steely strength was no longer hidden within. "Or is it acceptable for you but not for others?"

Janet flushed beet red, her hands on her hips, as she glared at the younger woman. "Oh, you think you can be brave now because you have the backing of Seamus O'Rourke and hope to trap one of his sons into marriage? Mark my words. No man wants used goods. No man wants a woman who is a tease and a flirt but who will never be able to satisfy him." She took a step forward to poke Lorena in her shoulder, her blue eyes glowing with acrimony. "No man wants to saddle himself with a lifetime's worth of obligation. For that's all you'd ever be—an obligation. A duty. A chain around his neck that he'll only dream of breaking free of."

Lorena tilted her chin up, standing as stiff as a board, as she fought panic at the older woman's words that stung as fiercely as anything her mama had ever spewed at her. "You're jealous because you have no idea what life can be like with a man who loves like an O'Rourke." She smiled in a cunning way, her smile broadening as Janet Davies stared at her in horror at the thought Lorena had already won an O'Rourke man's love.

"You do realize you're his fourth choice?" Janet said with a harsh indrawn breath, her hands clenched at her sides. "First was Aileen, then Ardan's bride—that witch in the kitchen." She glowered as she turned toward the café and considered Deirdre. "Can you imagine how much he was unmanned by having two women stolen by his brothers? And then that woman in Saint Louis didn't even want him and left him with a bastard child." She looked Lorena up and down and shrugged. "I suppose he'll take what he can get. You're better than having to raise his brat alone. Or with his wet nurse."

Lorena gazed at her, momentarily struck dumb at her hurtful words.

"I can see you didn't fully think through how unwanted you truly are. It's always shocking to realize how little value we bring to another's life. Or how unimportant we truly are." Glancing around the bookstore, she shrugged. "You'll fail at this and at your attempt to marry an O'Rourke. Your mother knew you were a failure. Your sister knows you're a failure, and so does your uncle. No man wants a failure." She turned on her heels, sauntering away with a breezy wave.

Lorena watched her departure, feeling as though she had just been sucker punched. She turned toward a window and fisted her hands together, digging her fingernails into her palms, berating herself for feeling again. However, the icy numbness she had clung to had melted away, and she was unable to remain impassive, stoic, and untouched by the hurtful comments of those around her. Nor could she ignore her racing heart and rising panic that an O'Rourke would hear about Lorena's boasting.

A giggle sounded in the doorway, and her gaze jerked in that direction. "That was entertaining, although you should have told her off at the end," Maggie said, as she stood with a basket. She held it up and shrugged. "You missed the midday meal, and Mum worried you'd go hungry."

Lorena rubbed at her stomach, shaking her head. "I can't imagine eating right now." Flushing, she murmured, "How much did you hear?"

Shrugging, Maggie said, "Enough to know you made her believe you and Declan are a couple." Her eyes widened. "Are you?"

Lorena closed her eyes in defeat, as her shoulders sagged. "No, of course we aren't. Your brother has taken pity on me because your father has commanded it of him, by coming here and helping me arrange books. He's also a bit of a guard dog."

Maggie perked up at that last sentence. "Guard dog?" A wry smile spread. "I've learned my brothers never act like that unless they're interested in the woman."

Rolling her eyes and then her shoulders, Lorena began to pace. "Don't start imagining things, Maggie. Declan's been kind. Kinder than I thought he would be." She rubbed at her temples. "Kinder than I deserve."

The younger woman grabbed Lorena's arm and held her still, waiting until Lorena met her gaze. "You don't believe that nonsense that viper spouted at the end? About men and what they want?" Maggie shook her head and let out an exasperated huff of air. "She's a miserable old spinster, who's never known love, who now has to put up with your pompous portly uncle so she won't starve."

Against her will, a smile burst forth, and Lorena giggled. "*Pompous portly?*"

Maggie shrugged again, looking pleased with herself. "I've spent a little time with that captain. He has a marvelous way with words."

Lorena freed herself from Maggie's hold to perch on a stool. "I thought you'd have no trouble with Seamus as your father."

"With tellin' tales and the like?" For a moment, Maggie sounded as Irish as any member of her family, and Lorena marveled at her ability to mimic those around her. Raising her hands to shove loose strands of her auburn hair back into her bun, Maggie made a noncommittal face. "I can tell a story, but the captain has a way of bringing words alive. And he's so much fun to listen to." She smiled again, as she looked around. "Are you ever very busy?"

Lorena paused a moment. "Yes, generally as a stage is about to depart. Dunmore helpfully informed me that there are no bookstores in Helena or Virginia City, and I'm attempting to spread the word. As travelers learn of that fact, they visit to find a new book or two to bring with them. Or they realize they shouldn't have left their Bibles behind."

Maggie perked up at the mention of Dunmore. "Dunmore's back?"

Lorena turned away to hide her smile, on the pretense of dusting the binding of a book. "Yes, he visited last evening, as I was about to close up. I thought you knew he had returned."

Maggie frowned and furrowed her brows. "No. I hate when he's away." She forced a smile as she looked at Lorena, a woman she considered family, although no joy reached her eyes. "If Dunmore told you that, then it's true. He doesn't lie."

Stilling, Lorena watching Maggie in wonder. "How remarkable it must be to have such faith in another." She watched as Maggie shrugged. "What do you think of my plan? I'm going to write up an announcement and hang it in public places. As long as the proprietors will allow me to."

Maggie brightened, her attention turned to Lorena's goal of drumming up more business. "You should have a flyer for the store, the hotel, the café, and the Bordello."

Gasping, Lorena shook her head. "I could never, ... never go to the Bordello. Presume to ... to ..."

Maggie waved away her concern. "Oh, you know the Madam from when Phoebe was hurt. She's a nice woman and a friend to all of us O'Rourkes." Shaking her head, she murmured, "Don't bother protesting you're not an O'Rourke. You've been taken in by Da and Mum, so you are as good as an O'Rourke to townsfolk."

"*As good as* doesn't mean I'm actually an O'Rourke." She paused, stilling her movement around the room to dust around books, as she saw Maggie watching her with concern. "What is it?"

"Is that it?" When Lorena stared at her with complete befuddlement, Maggie whispered, "Is that why you want Declan? To be one of us?"

Paling, Lorena fought a shiver. "Declan is a friend. Only a friend, Maggie. He ... I'll never marry him."

Maggie firmed her chin, staring at Lorena with disappointment. "And why wouldn't you marry Declan? Do you think you're too good for him?" Maggie shook her head. "What is wrong with you Mortimer sisters?" She stood with her blue eyes blazing and her hands on her hips, as she faced Lorena.

"I won't answer for my sisters. For my part, I suffered in the past, and I know I'll never ... It's me, Maggie, not Declan," she whispered, her voice barely audible. "Any woman would be fortunate to deserve such a man."

Her ire evaporating as rapidly as it had appeared, Maggie studied Lorena, as though she were attempting to determine how to cure her of an illness. "But *you* don't believe you deserve him. That's what you're saying." Maggie paused a long moment, as the silence between them was prolonged. "Someday, Lorena, you will have to face what haunts you. You deserve more than reading about a full and satisfying life in a book."

Lorena watched her leave, tears dripping down her cheeks, as she feared such courage would always elude her.

P hoebe rested in bed after her sister's visit. She knew she should rise, don a fresh dress, and visit Eamon. However, a lassitude filled her, and all she wanted to do was rest, as she contemplated her future. Rather than a bleak future filled with duty and strife and devoid of joy, she saw a kaleidoscope of happy moments. Eamon holding her close. Eamon smiling at her with love and pride. Eamon kissing the head of their baby, uncaring if their babe were a boy or a girl. Always Eamon.

A tear trickled out, as she held a hand low over her belly. She wanted a few more moments to hold the miracle of her surprise to herself before she sought him out. A few more moments to marvel that her body was capable of sheltering life. Although she knew Maggie would roll her eyes at her, as this was basic biology, this was a miracle to Phoebe.

The door latch sounded, and she looked over her shoulder to see Eamon standing, his hands fisted at his side.

"Love?" she asked.

"You're dying," he rasped. "You're dyin', an' you don't know how to tell me." His blue eyes shone with terror as he stared at her.

She rolled over so quickly in bed that she tangled herself in her dress and landed with a *thump* on the floor. "Ouch! No!" She sighed with relief when he pulled her up and wrapped his arms around her. "Hold me, Eamon. Just hold me."

"I'll hold you forever. I swear I won't let anyone take you from me," he vowed. "Don't leave me."

"Oh, my love, forgive me."

He pushed her away, his hands bracketing her face, as he stared fiercely into her eyes. "Never. I'll never forgive you if you leave me." Tears threatened as he whispered, "Don't make me suffer as Da suffered."

Raising her hands, she covered his mouth and shook her head. "*Shh*, you precious man. I'm not dying. I'm going to have our baby."

Eamon stilled, as though she spoke in a foreign tongue. Shaking his head, he stared at her for long moments, as though attempting to discern if she spoke the truth. When she nodded and smiled with a deep glow, he groaned and tugged her to him. "Oh, my precious girl. My beautiful wife." He held her so tightly that she squeaked. "Never scare me like that again. *Jaysus!*" He released her only enough to capture her lips in a passionate kiss. "A baby. We're to have a baby."

"Aye," she murmured, mimicking him. "A little one to play with his or her cousins. To swaddle with our love."

"Always, my darlin'. Always."

CHAPTER 7

The following afternoon, Declan paused outside the bookstore, lifting his face up to the soft rays of the sun. He knew that, too soon, it would be hot, and he'd have no wish to linger in the sunlight. His mind wandered, and he thought about his son, contented and always cheerful, currently under the care of Samantha, Maggie and his mum.

Thankfully Samantha was adapting to life among the O'Rourkes and enjoyed working with his mum and sister, although she preferred to avoid much contact with his brothers. Samantha seemed willing to stay here, working as a nanny, and sleeping in the makeshift nursery in the big house, even after Gavin was weaned. Declan smiled as he thought of his son, Gavin, who was blooming under all the attention from everyone in the family.

With a contented sigh, Declan acknowledged he'd made the right decision returning home.

As he was about to enter the small establishment, he heard a raised female voice. Recognizing it as the youngest Mortimer sister's snippy tone, he decided not to interrupt their conversation, although he couldn't help but overhear the one-sided conversation.

"You're pathetic, Lo. Starting up a business destined to fail. And then enticing an O'Rourke who has no interest in you to sit on a stool all day long as though you needed protection?" Winnifred said in a taunting voice. "It's worse than embarrassing. If there's a Mortimer sister who needs protection, it isn't you."

Declan strained to hear Lorena's reply, but all he heard were a few muffled syllables.

"Oh, that's rich," Winnifred pronounced in a loud carrying voice. "As though you're forced to have an attractive man sit and wait on you because his father demanded it. You're pathetic, and you know it. First you let Mama boss you around. And now you let Mr. O'Rourke."

Another murmur came and then a slap and a shriek. Deciding he'd heard enough, Declan entered the library, clearing his throat. Any attempt at a smooth conciliatory statement was lost the moment he saw the reddened mark on Lorena's cheek. "You'd dare strike your sister?" he demanded, as he glared at Winnifred, blocking the exit.

"She deserved it. She had no right to speak to me in such a manner."

"If anyone deserved it, it was you," Declan said in a low menacing voice. "For some reason, you believe that those around you will always accept your tantrums and your abuse. One day you will go too far, and you will be alone. And then you will understand what true misery is."

"I will never be alone, you buffoon. I am not the sort of woman who will ever be lonely." Winnifred held her head high, showcasing her elegant neck and beautiful face.

"You might have an allure now, but that will fade. And, as it does, few will have patience with your spitefulness." He stepped aside to approach Lorena, who now held a hand to her cheek. "Lorena, let me see it." He waited until she lowered her hand before softly touching her cheek. When she hissed, he glared at her sister. "Be useful for once and find some ice."

Winnifred stomped her foot in agitation. "I have better things to do than be your errand girl." She stormed away.

Declan ran his thumb over the reddened area. "Will she find ice?"

At the embarrassed look in Lorena's eye, he sighed. "Come. Let's close up for a little while and return home. Mum and Maggie will help."

"Winnie never likes to be ignored. And you focusing on me is the worst insult."

Declan smiled. "She doesn't deserve my attention." His smile broadened as Lorena flushed at the implication she did deserve it. "Come. Let's get you home and cared for."

"It's just a slap," she protested. "I've had worse."

He froze, his easy cajoling disappearing at her careless statement. *"Worse?"* He shook his head. "I pray never again." Dropping his hand from her cheek, he grabbed her hand. "Come." For the entire short walk to his parents' home, he held her hand. Although it garnered a few looks, he refused to allow her to feel any more alone than she already did.

After ushering her inside, he called for his sister. "Maggie," he said, when she appeared from her upstairs bedroom. "Can you ensure Lorena is well?"

Maggie looked at Lorena and frowned. "Did someone hit you?"

When Lorena remained resolutely silent, Declan murmured, "Winnifred." At Maggie's hiss of disgust, he nodded. "Aye. I'm to find ice. I'll be back." He squeezed Lorena's shoulder and then Maggie's before rushing away.

Lorena sat in the O'Rourke kitchen, battling a profound mortification. "There's no need to fuss," she whispered. "I'll be fine. A cold cloth should suffice."

"If Declan wants ice, then he'll find ice," Maggie said.

When Mary walked in, Lorena closed her eyes in defeat, and Maggie summarized what little she knew. At Mary's sounds of distress, Lorena wished she could dig a hole and hide in it. Anything to save her from their pitying stares. "It's nothing. Like I said to Declan ..." This time she bit her tongue.

"Like you said to Declan, *you've suffered worse?*" Mary asked, a too-knowing look in her gaze. "I've always wondered about all you've suffered, lass. And now that you're no longer following Winnifred's lead and her schemes, it makes sense she's quite angry with you. And lashing out. For she hopes you'll get back in line and do as she wants."

"I'm not her doll," Lorena hissed and closed her eyes. "For too long, it was easier to placate her—and Mama—than to protest."

"Aye, 'tis the way with a bully," Mary said. "But it eats away at your soul, little by little, does it not?" She shrugged, as she held a cold cloth to Lorena's cheek and then sat, wrapping an arm around the younger woman's waist and urging her to rest her uninjured cheek on Mary's shoulder. "I found that to be the truth with my second husband. A brute of a man. Nothin' like my Seamus."

"Few are like Mr. O'Rourke," Lorena whispered. "Or you."

"Ah, that might be true, but it doesn't mean you won't find a man who treasures you," Mary said, gently rocking Lorena, as though she were a wee babe in need of coddling. "We all need a little tenderness, Lorena. It's not a sign of weakness but of strength."

"I wasn't raised to believe that, Mrs. O'Rourke."

"How many times must I ask you to call me Mary? You're one of the family now, Lorena," Mary said, a soft note of admonishment in her voice. "You'll be family no matter what happens."

"I don't understand," Lorena whispered, her eyes closing, as she felt secure and protected for the first time in so long.

"I know. Perhaps one day you will."

Declan raced away from town toward the foothills that bracketed the backside of town. Knocking on the door, he paused, waiting to see if the icehouse proprietor, Mr. Crain, was here. After a moment, the door opened, and the man stood with a curious frown. "Aye?" He sighed at the sight of Declan. "An O'Rourke."

"Yes, I am, an' I'm in need of ice." He frowned when Mr. Crain shut the door.

"I don't have none for you, lad."

Declan hit the closed door with his fist, but it didn't budge. After a moment, he raced away in the direction of the levee. "A.J.!" he called out, when he approached the captain's steamboat, finding the captain on land. "Have any ships arrived in the past few days?"

Tipping his hat back and swiping at his forehead, A.J. huffed out a breath, sitting on a crate he'd helped to carry off the steamboat. "Yes, sonny, the *G.A. Thompson* arrived yesterday." He put a hand on his hip, as he stared at the younger man he considered a cousin. "What's he brought to town that I didn't?"

"Ice," Declan said, his blue eyes blazing with fury. "For some reason, Crain won't sell me any."

"Ah, well, I'm friends with the captain of the *Thompson*. Give me a minute." A.J. sauntered away, calling out a greeting and invoking laughter at his approach to the other steamboat's crew.

Declan shook his head as it seemed that, wherever the man went, he was greeted with smiles and good humor. He watched as A.J. motioned with his hands and then pointed in Declan's direction. After a few more minutes, A.J. walked back in his direction. "Well?" Declan asked.

"They have some ice in their stores. Found a last bit of it a few days ago." He scratched at his head. "They'll bring it to you once they carve off a piece." He settled on the crate again, clamping his jaw down as though he were smoking his pipe. "Why'd that man Crain deny you ice? You know every boat comes in with ice this time of year, an' we're eager to sell it."

Declan shrugged. "I don't know. He seemed upset at the sight of me. Said my name as though it were a curse."

A.J. tapped at his knee. "Well, not everyone in town's gonna like you and your family, sonny. There are always those who'll be jealous." He nodded in the direction of the boardwalk and a pompous-looking man with a protruding belly in a cranberry-colored waistcoat. "That man's a *baffoon* if I've ever seen one."

"A baboon or a buffoon?" Declan asked. "And he's Lorena's uncle."

"Poor girl, sufferin' as she does with her youngest sister, and has a man like that as her uncle." A.J. continued to glare at the portly man. "An' he's both."

With a frown in Chaffee's direction, Declan focused on A.J. "How do you know Winnifred is difficult?"

Shaking his head as though he were speaking to a simpleton, A.J. kicked at the crate across from him. "Sit. Might as well be comfortable while you wait." He met Declan's impatient gaze. "Anyone with eyes can see that youngest sister's nothin' but trouble. An' she's got her eyes on her eldest sister. Wants to lead her into temptation. An' I don't mean the good kind." A.J. shook his head. "Workin' down here at the levee, I hear all kinds of blatherin'. Most of it I ignore. But when the men started talkin' about there bein' new competition for the Bordello, an' the new arrival of a red-haired woman to bring them comfort, well, I took notice."

"Where?" Declan asked, canting forward. "The Daybreak?" At A.J.'s nod, Declan shook his head. "Chaffee thinks he'll have his niece be a Temptress?" He glowered in the direction Chaffee had been standing.

"From what I hear, he ain't got much choice. He's runnin' out of money. Not much use for a lawyer with expensive tastes in this town. An' men don't have legal problems here like they do in towns like Virginia City or Helena."

"Then why is he here?" Declan whispered. "It makes no sense."

A.J. huffed out a breath, although, for once, no humor lit his expression. "Well, we know it ain't for familial love. He wouldn't know what that was if a rattler bit him on his ass." He smiled as Declan snorted. "I've heard of a man called Bergeron." When Declan froze, A.J. nodded. "He's bidin' his time for that man to show up."

"Jacques," Declan whispered. "He's Lucien's and Henri's uncle. The brother to the man my mother married, after she was left behind in Montreal." He paused as A.J. continued to study him. "The man who will do anything to have Maggie."

A.J. chortled out a laugh. "Ah, lad, that's where you again prove you know nothin' about women. For, if you did, you'd know that stage-coach driver will do anythin' for that sweet girl." He paused. "But I'd be on your guard. More is afoot than we know."

Declan nodded, biting back what more he would have said, as he rose and accepted a hunk of ice from the kind stranger, who promptly left. "Thank you, A.J. I must return and get this to Lorena."

With a twinkle in his brown eyes, A.J. smiled. "Of course you do, sonny. You can't keep your ladylove waitin'. An' it's important you show her how much you care."

"No! It's not like that." When he remained here, water dripping onto his boot from the melting ice, A.J. staring at him as though he were a fool, Declan heaved out a breath. "I have to go. But it isn't what you think." He raced away, refusing to give any credence to A.J.'s impertinent comments.

~

Lorena sat at the kitchen table, a cold cloth to her cheek, as she tickled Gavin's feet while he sat on Maggie's lap. Samantha had puttered around the kitchen for a little while, scurrying away when the youngest group of O'Rourke sons entered. Lorena realized Samantha always disappeared when O'Rourke men other than Declan or Seamus were present. As for Gavin, the majority of his time was spent with family.

Gavin reached forward to grab the cloth, scraping her reddened cheek. With an unbidden hiss, Lorena grimaced. "No, love," she whispered, as she arched away from his touch. When his lip quivered, she relented and gave him the damp cloth. At his squeal of delight, she smiled, wincing again at the pain in her face.

"Gavin will overcome his momentary disappointment," Declan said in a soft voice.

Her head jerked up, as she hadn't heard him enter. "Declan," she gasped, her gaze taking in his quiet presence and the soft tenderness in his gaze, as he watched her interacting with his son. "I'm fine."

"Don't lie," he murmured, moving to the countertop and pulling out a sharp knife. He whittled away a piece of ice, wrapping it in a new square of cloth, before moving to the table. He held it out, setting it with the utmost care against her reddened cheek.

71

"Heaven," she breathed, as the coldness seeped into her skin and soothed the deep ache. When his long fingers stroked her other cheek, she looked into his eyes, swallowing once before breathing, "Thank you."

"You're welcome, Lo," he murmured, dropping his hand and reaching for Gavin. Maggie rose, scurrying from the room, and he settled in Maggie's place.

"She didn't have to leave," Lorena protested, her hand holding the ice-filled compress to her cheek.

Chuckling, Declan kissed the top of Gavin's head. "Aye, she did. She knew we needed a few moments together." When he paused, staring deeply at her, she ducked her head, breaking eye contact with him. "Why are you embarrassed?"

Shaking her head, she whispered, "I'm not embarrassed." She dared to look at him through a sheen of tears, making her eyes appear the color of jade. "I'm ashamed. My own sister hit me. Treated me with such disregard." She lost her battle with her deep emotions, and a tear coursed down her cheek.

Declan settled Gavin in his arms, as the boy tumbled into sleep, and focused all his attention on the woman sitting beside him. "That is her shame, Lorena, not yours."

She shook her head. "It's always been mine. Any problem we've ever had has always been my fault." She exhaled a deep, shaky breath. "It's all the worse now because I won't do what she expects me to do."

He rocked Gavin in his arms, the motion soothing him as much as it did his son. "You mean, you won't be her puppet?" At her startled gaze, he shrugged. "I know what bullies are and how they act. And your youngest sister is a bully, Lorena."

Lorena readjusted her hold on the compress, whispering, "She's a lot like Mama."

Reaching forward, he gripped the hand that she held fisted on the table. "Then I'd give thanks you're nothin' like your mama." He met her shocked gaze. "For, if she was like Winnifred, she wasn't a nice woman." He paused. "I'm sorry. I shouldn't speak against your mother. I never knew her."

"No one ever speaks against Mama," Lorena whispered. "And I think that's part of the problem. None of us dared. And we should have dared. For she was cruel and vindictive and controlling." She closed her eyes. "And I allowed her to ruin my life."

Declan made a sound of disagreement. "From where I'm sitting, your life isn't ruined. You've a business, friends who are like family, and you're still young yet." He stared at her a long moment. "You've your life ahead of you. Count your blessings." He rose, taking Gavin with him and leaving her alone in the kitchen.

Lorena sat in deep contemplation, as she thought about her relationship with her mother. She never would have thought herself capable of criticizing her mother. However, in the past year, she had found an intrinsic strength she hadn't known she had. And a sense of worth her mother had hoped she'd never discover. "Oh, Mama," she whispered, as she held the now sodden compress to her face, "why couldn't you have loved me as I was? As I am?" She battled a deep desire that she'd known a mother's love like that of Mary O'Rourke and wondered how different her life would be now, if only she'd been shown love, rather than contempt.

A few days later, Declan entered the kitchen, pausing as he heard peals of laughter coming from the living room area. He poked his head around the doorway from the kitchen, his breath catching at the sight of Lorena holding Gavin high in the air, as she beamed up into his chubby face, while he chortled with glee. Mum, Maggie, and Samantha were in the room, all sewing or knitting, as they told stories and enjoyed each other's company. Feeling like an intruder, Declan had no desire to interrupt their afternoon together, although he yearned for such moments with Gavin. He didn't have nearly as much time as he would like with his son since returning home.

Focusing again on Lorena, Declan caught his breath at the adoration in her gaze, as she now held Gavin on her lap, him facing the room and playing with a spoon she held. He tried to master the art of putting it in his mouth but continually missed. He drooled on her fingers and had drool dripping down his jaw too. Rather than be upset, Lorena soothed him and pulled out a clean cloth to swipe at his face, allowing him to gnaw on her finger. "I think the little man is teething," she murmured.

"Aye," Mary said, as she glanced in her grandson's direction. "If it were winter, 'twould be easier for the lad. We could freeze cloths outside, and he could suck on them. But 'tisn't possible in this Montana summer."

"You'll be all right, Gavin darling," Lorena soothed, as she kissed his head. "Soon you'll have big strong teeth, and you'll be able to eat food, like we do."

"Yum," Maggie said in a sing-song voice that made Gavin giggle. "Cake that Mum or Deirdre makes. That'll be your favorite."

Declan continued to watched Lorena with his son, battling a deep yearning that he had met a woman like her rather than Magnolia. That Gavin would have a mother who loved and cherished him, rather than no one. Unbidden, a vision of his ideal life floated through his mind. Coming home every day to a house filled with laughter, joy, and love. Where his children never doubted how much they were adored. He sighed. Where Gavin never doubted how much he was cherished.

Shaking his head, Declan turned to silently exit the house. He sat on the back steps, sitting in the shade, as the image of his perfect life taunted him. Teased him with all that he desired and all that he still did not have. All that he feared he would never have.

Taking another deep breath, he finally admitted to himself that, in this dream, he saw Lorena greeting him when he arrived home. Lorena with children around her, laughing and smiling. Lorena working at her store, discussing whatever interested her that day, as he found a reason to spend time in her presence.

Always Lorena.

CHAPTER 8

A few weeks had passed since the opening of her bookstore, and Lorena was now accustomed to Declan's company. Although he had promised she wouldn't know he would be present, on the second day of business, he had begun chatting with her about an array of topics and hadn't stopped chattering since. Never in her life had she met someone who matched her inquisitive mind or who thrilled at her desire for constant learning.

She looked up from her perch on a stool to smile at the captain, who had taken an interest in the O'Rourkes wandering into her store. "Hello, sir."

He smiled at her and doffed his cap, sending his too long hair in all directions. After he smoothed it down with a chuckle, he continued to smile at her impishly. "I thought the magpie would be here."

"I'm afraid I don't have a magpie as a pet. I can't imagine such a bird would be content in a cage."

"It's A.J., miss, or Mr. A.J., if ye feel a need to be formal with your customers." He scratched at his head. "I can't imagine any bird likes bein' caged, do you?" At her shake of her head, he chortled. "I meant your young suitor. Sonny."

"*Sonny?*" Lorena asked, before sputtering out, "*Suitor?* I have no suitor, sir. I'll never marry. I'm a spinster."

"You young'uns have such odd notions about yourselves. I might not look old, but I sure do feel it sometimes. Spent too much time as a river rat." He looked at her speculatively. "An' I know a thing or two about courtship. How else do you think I married my Bessie?" When Lorena continued to stare at him dazedly, he said, "That O'Rourke boy, Declan, whether he knows it or not, he's got his eye on you." He nodded with delight when she gasped. "An' it appears you have yours on him."

"I have no such thing!" Lorena held a hand to her heaving chest, suddenly feeling light-headed and out of breath. "He spends time here merely because his father instructed him to."

"No man finds delight in a woman because his papa orders it. A man tends to become ornery when commanded to do something he doesn't want to do." When she remained silent, he asked, "You tellin' me that he doesn't like bein' here? That he wishes he were somewhere else?"

"No, it's never like that." She flushed. "He's a friend, Mr. A.J. Nothing more."

A.J. wandered to the crates that acted like bookshelves, perusing the titles. "I've always liked a good adventure story. Do you have anything I might like?"

She approached with a small stack of books by the publisher Beadle. "Have you read these?"

He flipped through them, picking one of the dime novels. "I like the sounds of this one. Intrigue. Murder. A chance for redemption." He placed it on the counter. "How much?"

"Fifty cents." She met his raised eyebrow. "Shipping isn't cheap."

"Robbery ain't cheap either," he muttered, as he slapped two coins on the counter. "An' next time, tell a customer it's *two bits*. You'll sound more like one of us an' not so uppity."

"*Uppity?*" she asked, her back straightening with affront.

He chuckled as he picked up his book. "Aye, uppity." He looked around. "An' don't defend your price. If I don't want to pay it, I'll turn tail an' walk away." He waved his hand in the air, as though to indicate moving away. "Take pride in what you've built, miss. I'm sure your mama would be proud of you."

Lorena froze at the words, her smile forced. "I wish you were correct, sir. But I fear you would be mistaken." She cleared her throat. "I don't come from a family like the O'Rourkes."

A.J. tapped the spine of his book against the counter as he studied her. "Now, miss, who does?" He shook his head. "I ain't met a family that big but that *congevial* in all my travels."

She stilled, her gaze focused on him. "*Congevial?* Do you mean *convivial? Congenial?*"

He nodded. "Aye, you're as smart as Sonny at playing my game. My Bessie would love you." He sighed. "And your mama's a fool for not seein' what a gem you are." He paused as he gazed at her in an assessing manner. "My bet is that she only focused on your beauty. Thought your brains were a burden, not a blessin'."

Her mouth dropped open, as she stared at him. "How did you know that?"

Shrugging, A.J. said, "Doesn't take no genius after spendin' a miserable few minutes with that youngest sister of yours. If she's anythin' like your mama ..." He shook his head. "There are those who are afraid of intelligence an' those who know beauty only gets you so far. You need brains too." He winked at her. "Although bein' pretty ain't a bad thing."

Against her will, she burst out laughing. "You're incorrigible, aren't you?"

He puffed out his chest and hooked the fingers of one hand through his suspenders. "Aye. It's harder than it looks, an' it's taken a lifetime of practice." When she laughed again, he smiled. "You need to laugh more, miss." He raised his book. "I'll be back soon to swap this one out. Don't linger too late, miss." He held his book up again in a salute, as he sauntered away, whistling a jaunty tune.

Declan sat at the family dinner table, waiting for his siblings to arrive, while casting furtive glances at the kitchen door. He hadn't seen Lorena enter, but, after she had sent him away, insistent that she was fine in her own store, he didn't want to appear too overbearing. However, he knew he wouldn't be at ease until she had returned and was seated down the table from him.

The younger lads entered, chattering a mile a minute about the goings on at the levee. Declan caught Bryan's youthful voice excitedly telling the tale of a fight and a man falling into the Missouri. "They thought he'd float, but he was weighted down with gold from the mining camps," Bryan said, his green eyes lit with wonder at the thought. "Men dove in to save him in an attempt to recover the gold!"

"Sure you're makin' that up, lad," Seamus said with an indulgent look, as he beheld his youngest son.

"No, Da, I swear!" Bryan said with youthful enthusiasm, now sitting on his knees as he prepared to expound on his tale. He beamed as his older brothers Oran and Henri nodded to give credence to what he said. "He fell in with the most wondrous *plop* and started screaming about his boots. That they were loaded with gold dust, and he'd drown."

"He was sinking pretty fast," Oran muttered.

"Ol' A.J. threw in an empty cask for him to tie himself to, and that began to sink also!" Bryan said, acting like he was sinking under the table. "But it had enough air in it to keep him afloat."

"Who got his boots?" Declan asked, inadvertently charmed by his youngest brother's story.

"A.J. got one, and the man kept the other. Seemed only fair the captain would receive one boot, after saving the man's life."

Declan shared an amused look with his da, hiding a smile behind a sip of tea. "Aye, only fair." He glanced at his mother and Maggie, chatting quietly by the stove. "Mum, how long 'til supper?"

"Oh, only a few more minutes, although I'd prefer to wait for Lorena and your brothers." She pushed a strand of hair behind one ear. "'Tisn't like Lorena to be so late."

Declan rose. "I'll go. Ensure she hasn't started reading a book and forgotten the time." He winked at his mum, slipping out the back door. Sniffing at the air, he frowned at his neighbors lighting their chimneys in the summer. Usually only a soft hint of woodsmoke lingered in the air from the stoves, but a heavy scent permeated the evening breeze. He whistled as he turned from the backyard and headed in the direction of the bookstore.

He looked up at the sound of a crash, his pace faltering at the sight of a flame kissing up the front doorway of the bookshop. "Fire!" he screamed. "Fire!" he bellowed over and over, as he raced to the store. Just as he arrived, a beam fell, blocking the front entrance.

He ran to the back, noting the flames remained at the front of the store, although he knew they would spread quickly with the flammable books and dry wood framing of the store. He jerked on the windows, swearing when he remembered they didn't open. "Lorena! Lo!" He was about to break a window with a fist covered with his jacket when Kevin sprinted around the side of the building with an ax, Niall on his heels.

Kevin swung the ax a few times, easily splintering the flimsy wood. Niall and Declan kicked at it, making a large enough opening for Declan to ease through. He heard his brothers continue to work on widening the opening, as he entered the smoke-filled space. "Lo!" he called out and then coughed, as his lungs filled with smoke.

Glancing at the front of the store, he prayed she wasn't there, as flames licked the ceiling, and it threatened to collapse any moment. As he approached the counter, he saw her huddled behind it, her shawl over her head. "Lo," he gasped. "Come, love."

Unconscious, she fell toward him like a rag doll. Catching her, he grunted, as he lifted her into his arms, ducking over her to protect her from flying embers and falling debris, as something hard hit his back. Smoke filled his gaze, and he felt as though he were being roasted alive from the heat. After a few halting steps, he approached the now widened opening, handing Lorena out, trusting one of his brothers would be there to take her.

When his arms were free, he stumbled outside, tripping on a piece of wood and falling to his knees, as a coughing fit overcame him. He watched, tears streaming down his soot-covered cheeks, as Ardan ran with Lorena in his arms in the direction of his parents' house.

"Lo," he rasped, sighing with pleasure when Lucien pressed a cup of water to his lips. After his throat was soothed, he whispered again, "Lo."

Seamus passed off his bucket to another man and knelt in front of Declan. "You know your mum and sisters will look after her. Let's get you cleaned up, and then perhaps you'll be able to see her too." Seamus heaved him up, easing a shoulder below Declan's to keep him from falling. After Lucien supported Declan on the other side, he walked toward his parents' house.

With a glance over his shoulder, Declan murmured, "Will any of it be saved?"

"Nay," Seamus said, with a murmur of regret. "I'm only thankful we won't be havin' a funeral."

Declan shivered at the thought, leaning heavily on his da, as he made his slow way back to his family's home.

"Declan!" Maggie said, as he stumbled into the kitchen with his father's aid. "Sit down, and let me look at you."

"Nay, Maggie, help Lorena. She's much worse than I am," he gasped, as he winced, sitting down and arching forward, so his back wouldn't touch the chair.

"Oh, you *eejit*," Maggie snapped. "She's upstairs with Mama and Nora. They'll call me if they need help, but I suspect all she needs is time to overcome the smoke she inhaled." She looked at her brother, shaking and pale in the chair reserved for their father, and reached for a pair of scissors. "Whereas you, you're a mess."

Ignoring his protests, she cut away his jacket, waistcoat, and shirt, nodding her thanks when Da helped strip them off Declan. "Oh, Dec," she breathed, as she saw the long line of singed flesh on his back. She reached forward, touching the very edge of the burn, stilling her movement when he hissed in a breath. "'Tis already blisterin'," she murmured.

"What can I do?" Seamus asked her.

"Find more ice," she said, as she bustled around the kitchen, opening up a portion of the pantry reserved for her herbs.

"Find A.J.," Declan gasped out, murmuring his thanks as Maggie handed him a cup of water. "He'll help you. Crain wouldn't sell me ice when I needed it for Lorena."

Seamus nodded, squeezing Declan's arm and then kissing Maggie's forehead. "I'll return as soon as I can."

Maggie boiled water for tea and placed a cold compress on his back. At his sharp inhalation, she whispered, "I'm sorry, Dec."

"Don't apologize for helpin' me, Maggie." He gazed at her in confusion. "I never realized you were a healer."

She shrugged. "I love it, but I only practice on family. I've had no formal training, and, with Chaffee running lose, he'd relish any reason he could find to sue me for harming someone."

"Bloody man," Declan gasped, as she rubbed honey over the wound. He shook his head when she handed him tea to drink. "I don't want anything hot just now, Mags. It hurts my throat."

"Drink it," she urged. "I've added honey to it too, and the tea will help with your pain. It's willow bark tea."

He gave a grunt of disgust but drank down the entire mug of acrid-tasting tea. "When can I see Lorena?"

"As soon as you are better," she soothed. "You'll do her no good if you're ailing as well, Declan." She looked to the back door at the clattering of footsteps. Their brothers entered, with soot-covered clothes and streaks of dirt on their cheeks. They reeked of smoke, and Maggie held her hands on her hips. "You're worse than any description I've ever read of chimney sweeps."

Bryan held his arms wide, his green eyes lit with delight. "I was in the bucket brigade!" He beamed at his older sister, as she ruffled his brown hair.

"Imp," she murmured. "Take care of Dec. He's a bad burn on his back and 'twill take time for it to heal."

81

Niall peered around Maggie to look at Declan's back, whistling in a breath. "What happened to you, Dec? I thought you got in and out unscathed."

Shrugging and then grimacing at the movement, Declan met his brothers' worried gazes. "So did I. I didn't feel a thing. Not until Da started helping me home. Then it felt like I had a poker searing my back." He shifted, as though that would help soothe the discomfort. "Still do."

"Da's gone for ice," Maggie murmured to the boys. "Clean up and be quiet. Mum and Nora are tending Lorena." Pointing to a pile of clean towels and clothes, she beamed at them, as they tiptoed from the kitchen to the backyard and the nearby stream. "Ah, peace. They'll be gone for a little while."

Chuckling and then coughing, Declan rasped out, "You're becoming proficient at managing all of us, Mags." He used the nickname Kevin had given her after her return two years ago.

"I'm learning from Mum," Maggie said with a wry smile. She urged him to lean forward, resting his head on his forearms. "I'm placing cool towels on your back. When Da returns, we'll use ice too."

"I'm fine, Mags," he whispered, his voice sleep thickened.

"Aye, an' I'm an Irish princess," she murmured, her hand stroking the thick black hair at his nape, as she listened to the easy cadence of his breathing when he slipped into a momentary slumber. She knew that, too soon, either pain or an O'Rourke would waken him. For now, she hoped he would rest and begin recovering from his injury.

Lurching awake, Declan sat up, immediately groaning, as the wound on his back pulled and felt like it burned all the way to his bones. He knew Maggie had muttered something about a blister and being a superficial burn due to his layer of clothes, but a deep throbbing began. Just as quickly, he thought of Lorena, and he pushed aside his own personal torment.

Rising, he paused a moment to regain his balance, before striding to the living room with the intention of finding her. He came to a clumsy halt when Eamon stepped in his path. "Let me pass," he whispered, his throat still smoke filled and raspy.

"No, Dec," Eamon said, Finn behind him. "Give Lorena time. Maggie, Mum, and Phoebe are still with her. Madam Nora had to return to the Bordello."

He rocked on his feet, collapsing to the sofa, as he listened for any sound from upstairs. When none came, he stared at them in dumbfounded confusion. "'Tis too quiet."

Finn smiled reassuringly. "There's no need for wailing or carrying on, Dec. She's alive still." He grunted when Eamon elbowed him in his side. "Maggie reassured us there was little risk of her suffering any long-term effects."

"But there's still a risk," Declan said, as he moved to heave himself up again.

Eamon rested a hand on his shoulder, crouching beside him. "Aye, there's always a risk. But they're caring for her. It's a small room, Dec, with little space for you."

Declan stared long and hard at his younger brother, who was already married. "Tell me, Eamon. When your Phoebe was injured, were you content to kick your heels outside her sickroom, or did you insist on being beside her?"

Eamon sighed and swore under his breath, before squeezing Declan's shoulder. "You're right. Come on, Dec. We'll make sure you get up the stairs without falling over."

Declan glared at the twins, but, when he rose on unsteady legs, he realized their concern was valid. With Finn in front and Eamon behind, Declan slowly walked up the stairs, perplexed at how out of breath he was when he made it to the top.

Finn softly knocked on the door, talking with Maggie for a moment. He turned, shook his head, urging Declan into their bedroom. "Come, Dec. They are helping her to wash up. When they're done, Maggie will come for us. Until then, lay down."

Declan groaned as he collapsed face-first onto his bed. "I hate sleeping on my stomach," he muttered. After a long moment, he pushed himself up, so he rested on his forearms and looked at his brothers. "I've never thanked you."

Finn and Eamon shared a perplexed glance. Called the twins, less than two years separated them, and they shared the same black hair and blue eyes. A few townsfolk had mixed them up, a common occurrence when they were boys. "Why would you thank us?" Eamon asked.

"For trying to look out for me in Saint Louis. For allowing me to act a fool. For still being my brothers." He waited a long moment before whispering, "I'm sorry."

Finn sat with a *thud* on the bed across from Declan's. "I'm sorry, Dec. I've thought and thought about it, but I've yet to discover a way to have prevented you from being fascinated by that woman."

"Evil witch," Eamon muttered.

Declan smiled and shook his head. "There's nothing either of you could have done. I was desperate for someone to care for me, and I never realized I was being played for a fool."

Eamon and Finn shared a long look. "Why'd you chase after her?" Eamon asked. His black hair was neatly trimmed, and his blue eyes shone with the contentment of a man who had everything he wanted in life.

Declan rested his head to one side on his pillow, so he was still able to speak with them. "She left me a letter. Telling me that she'd never loved me and that she doubted she'd ever love the child she would have. She said she hoped she'd find a decent orphanage where she was headed."

He met his brothers' aghast stares. "I remember you speaking with Andre Martin about New Orleans and thought it would be a place to search for her. I was right." He shuddered. "She and Andre were already trying to find someone who would buy the baby as soon as she gave birth."

"*Buy?*" Eamon whispered, as Finn swore under his breath.

"Aye," Declan said. He closed his eyes, as the distant scene replayed in his mind. "They were desperate for money. I suddenly realized she'd only ever wanted me for what I could give her. Never for who I was." He groaned as he moved, meeting his brothers' worried gazes. "And I suddenly realized I didn't care if that child was mine. I had to protect it from her. From whoever would buy a baby."

"What did you do?" Finn asked.

"I agreed to give them an exorbitant amount of money after the baby was born, as long as they gave the child to me." His eyes clouded. "Magnolia died in childbirth, and Andre thought the baby should die too, for causing her death. Thankfully the midwife saved Gavin and brought him to me. Somehow she'd heard of me."

"Did you pay Andre?" Eamon asked.

Declan shook his head. "Nay. I never saw Andre again. And I claimed Gavin as mine from the first day. And he is."

"Aye," Eamon whispered, Finn murmuring his agreement. "No one would doubt he's your lad."

Declan ignored the irony of the statement, as Gavin looked nothing like Declan. "Forgive me?" Declan asked. "I was mad with anger and grief ..." He closed his eyes. "Just filled with rage."

"I forgive you, Dec," Finn said.

"I do too," Eamon said, "although I'm still angry you forced us to come home to tell Mum and Da that you weren't comin' back and that you'd met a feckless lass." He rolled his eyes. "Thank God you have more sense this time around."

Declan lifted his head to stare at his brothers. "What are you talkin' about?"

Shrugging, Finn said, "Lorena of course." He bit off what more he would have said when Maggie poked her head into the room.

Her alert gaze took in Declan's bare back, frowning as she looked at his burn. "Dec, don't move. Wait for me, and then you can see Lorena." She looked at the twins. "Make him stay put." Her footsteps clattered away, and the sound of her returning a moment later calmed Declan's impatience. She held clean cloths and a jar. "I'll put a salve on your back and then cover you up."

She pulled the lid off her jar, using a spoon to spread the thick calendula ointment onto his skin. As he jerked in pain at her gentle ministrations, she murmured soothing sounds. "I'm sorry, but 'twill help you heal." When she was done, she set aside the jar and placed clean cloths over his back. After motioning Finn and Eamon over to hold the cloths in place, she urged Declan to sit up and wrapped large strips of cloth around his chest to keep everything from slipping off. "There," she said with a satisfied nod of her head. "That's good for now."

She gazed into his pain-dulled eyes. "Do you want to sleep or see Lorena?" She ignored Eamon's snort of amusement, as she focused on Declan.

"See Lorena," he said with a grunt, as he moved to stand.

Maggie gripped his arm and walked with him to the bedroom Lorena shared with Maggie and Winnifred, but now it served solely as a sickroom. Maggie and Winnifred would find other beds for the night. "She woke for a moment, but she's asleep again. Mama and Nora aren't worried because she woke. They believe she'll be fine." She let go of his arm, as he entered and collapsed onto the chair beside her bed.

Ignoring Maggie puttering around the small room, Declan focused on Lorena. On the ashen pallor of her skin. On her deep breaths. On her beautiful red hair fanned out around her head. He reached forward, tracing a finger through the silky locks, before caressing his fingers over her arm to clasp her fingers.

"Declan?" Maggie murmured, stroking a hand over his shoulder. "I'm sorry to interrupt, but I found a shirt for you to put on." She held out an oversize nightshirt. "It should be easy to slip on and off."

"Thanks, Mags," he said in a soft voice, releasing Lorena's hand and gingerly raising his arms up to pull on the shirt. "I never knew a burn could hurt this bad." He met his sister's worried gaze.

"Burns are the worst pain," she said. "Don't stay here too long. You need to rest and heal too." She kissed his forehead and slipped from the room, shutting the door behind her.

Declan immediately reached for Lorena's hand again, needing that connection with her. A little of his tension eased when he saw her relax at his contact. "I'm here, Lo. You're safe," he murmured. "I won't leave."

~

Declan looked toward the door that creaked open, as he sat at Lorena's bedside. "Niamh," he murmured. "Why are you here?" Lorena remained asleep, a peaceful expression on her face, as he sat beside her, praying for her to wake.

Staring at her brother, Niamh frowned. "Where else should I be?" She entered the room, bending over slightly to kiss his head. She sat in the empty chair beside him, stroking her hand down his arm and leaning against him, her head on his shoulder. "I'm sorry, Dec."

"Thanks," he said in a soft voice. "I keep thinking, over and over again, what I could have done to prevent a fire in her store." He rubbed at his head, grunting as the movement provoked pain.

"No one can prevent every calamity," she murmured. "Maggie said you were injured." Her gaze took him in, and she shook her head. "You look unharmed."

"I have a burn on my back. Hurts like the devil," Declan admitted. When she moved to lift his nightshirt to look at it, he shook his head. "Maggie has it covered in ointment and clean cloths. Best to leave it undisturbed."

"Oh, Declan," Niamh whispered. "I'm so sorry."

"I'm not," he said, as he looked at Lorena. "I would have done anythin' to keep her safe. To save her from ..." He shook his head, rather than voice the agonizing possibility of what could have befallen Lorena. "How are you here, Niamh? I thought you'd be home with your babes?"

"Da knew I wanted to see you. That I was mad with worry. He's with the lads." She leaned against him again, but more gently now that she knew about his injury. When she sensed the tension that continued to thrum through him, she murmured, "What is it?"

"I can't care like this, Niamh. Not again. Not so soon."

She pushed away to gaze into the startling blue eyes shared by so many O'Rourkes. "Oh, Dec," she whispered. "Of course you can." She swallowed. "Do you think it was easy for me to trust in Cormac's love? To have faith in my ability to choose a good man the second time, after choosing such a vile man the first?" Her hazel eyes were filled with torment for a moment.

"How did you overcome your doubts?" His gaze gleamed with his deep disillusionment.

She paused, focusing on Lorena for a long moment. "Cormac left, after I hurt him. And I realized what life without him would be like. Desolate. Devoid of the hope I'd begun to feel." She took a deep breath. "I had to come to believe that I was worth loving. An' that my love was worth receiving." She shook her head. "I'm not makin' any sense."

"No, you are," he whispered. "I've felt so worthless since Magnolia. She threw me away, as though I were as worthless as a piece of garbage. And she would have done the same to Gavin."

"Your son," Niamh said. "For, no matter what, he's yours."

Declan closed his eyes, as though suffering a body blow. "Aye, he's mine."

Niamh nudged him with her shoulder. "You've seen Cormac with my lads. You've seen how he loves them." At his nod and perplexed look, she murmured, "He's not father to either of them. Connor is."

"What?" Declan gasped. "I thought Cillian was Cormac's."

Shaking her head, Niamh whispered. "Nay. I was pregnant and didn't know it when I married my Cormac. I thought he'd leave me. Would want nothin' to do with me." She shared a chagrined smile with her brother. "I was a fool to ever doubt him. He's steadfast in his love. And our children will never know a life without a father's love. He's taught me so much about love and honor and loyalty."

She eased away to gaze at her brother, dressed in a plain nightshirt. She pointed. "This seems more like the Declan who I grew up with." At his frown, she explained. "You in your fancy clothes, even a waistcoat when you first arrived, was a surprise." She grinned at her lost brother, now home. "I never thought to see you dressed like a businessman, with your hair and beard cut short."

Declan grimaced and rubbed at his trimmed beard. "I, ah, I knew no woman would want the wild man. I needed to polish my appearance."

"No woman? Or no woman like Magnolia?" Niamh asked with a frown and a look of grave disapproval. "Do I seem disappointed in my husband dressed as a backwoodsman? Is Deirdre longing to shear Ardan with her kitchen scissors?" She shook her head, as she battled a giggle at the image of her sister-in-law attempting to tame her eldest brother's long mane and thick beard. "We don't esteem them for who they are out here." She waved her hand around at the external aspect of his appearance. "We love and admire them for who they *are.*"

Declan firmed his jaw and shook his head. "You don't know what it does, Niamh. To always be looked at with distaste."

"And cuttin' your hair and changin' your clothes put you in her favor?" Niamh challenged with a raised eyebrow. "If her love is that fickle, 'tisn't worth workin' for." She sat back with a *hmph*, as she crossed her arms over her chest. "You know you're worth more than that, Dec. You *know* it."

Declan closed his eyes for a moment, before nodding. "Aye. 'Twas easier believin' somethin' simple like a haircut could aid me in earnin' her love. I should never have even bothered tryin'. She was soulless, Niamh. How could I have ever wanted a woman like her?"

She gripped his hand. "How could I have married Connor?" She smiled softly at him. "I had to learn to forgive myself for making a terrible mistake, although I'll never regret my children. An' you must forgive yourself too. We make mistakes. We move on. And, if fate is kind, we learn and find a better person to love."

They sat for many minutes in quiet companionship. Finally Niamh murmured, "I was fortunate. Cormac believed in me. In us. He had always loved me." She looked at her brother and squeezed his hand. "I didn't have to convince him to care for me. And, in that, you have a harder task."

Declan nodded. "Aye, one I'm still tryin' to determine if it's worth fightin' for."

"Oh, 'tis worth it, Declan. You've known, long before the rest of us, that this life was not meant to be lived alone. You deserve to be happy with a woman who is proud to stand beside you. And for you to be proud to be beside her." She rose, kissing his head again. "I'm so glad you're home, Dec."

~

L orena stirred, her eyes weighted down, as though by heavy rocks. She struggled, fighting her way through the mist, until she cracked open her eyes, staring at the walls in the bedroom she shared with her sister and Maggie. A gentle light spilled in through the window, and a soft breeze ruffled the yellow curtains. Closing her eyes, she knew instinctively she was safe and began to slip back into sleep.

A loud snore jarred her awake, and she frowned at the unexpected noise. A snore? She turned her head with eyes slit open to gape at the sight of Declan asleep in Maggie's bed. He was on his side, with a pillow tucked up against his chest. "What are you doing here?" she breathed, gasping at the pain in her throat. Unbidden, a coughing fit overcame her, and she leaned on one arm, panting for breath.

"Lo!" Declan cried out, lurching up as he woke with a start. "Are you well? What do you need?" He reached for a glass of water, holding it to her lips, as he cupped the back of her head. "*Shh*, darlin', you're all right. No one will hurt you. You're fine."

She stared at him incredulously. "Of course I'm fine. I'm in my bedroom. Why are you sleeping here and not with the other boys?" She rubbed at her eyes. "Oh, why is my throat so dry, and why do my eyes feel like I have sandpaper in them?"

Declan stared at her with a deep sorrow. "Don't you remember, lass?" He waited, as she stared at him in confusion. He sat in the chair beside her bed with shoulders hunched in an oversize night-shirt that gave this moment a feeling of intimacy. As though they were much more than friends. "Rest, lass," he murmured, as he waited for her to ease onto her side again in bed. "There was a fire—"

"*Fire*," she breathed, her eyes widening with horror and fear. "I remember smoke." She closed her eyes, as Declan remained quiet, holding her hand. "And the front door was blocked with flames. I couldn't get out. And then …" She shrugged. "I remember nothing."

He swiped a hand over her hair, his thumb caressing her cheek. "By the time I got there, the front door was blocked outside by a fallen beam." His gaze swirled with panic, as he reenvisioned the scene. "Kevin came runnin' with an ax from the store, an' we hacked another opening." His thumb continued to play over her soft skin, reminding them both that she was alive and well.

She reached forward, her hand shaking, as it stroked his brows, brushing at a lock of ebony hair. "I'm fine. I'm here," she whispered.

His arms reached around her, gathering her up to haul her onto his lap with a groan. "Let me hold you," he pleaded. "I … I need to know you're well."

"You and your family saved me," she whispered into his ear, after she settled with her arms wrapped around his neck.

"If we hadn't, someone else would have," he murmured, holding her close.

She backed away, cupping his face in her palms. "No, Declan. Everyone else would have assumed I was already at your home. None would have searched for me." She bit her lip, as her eyes filled with tears. "My books?"

He shook his head, his thumb swiping at her tear. "I'm sorry, love. I focused on you. By the time I knew you were safe, there was no way to stop the fire or to save anything." He swallowed. "The building burned to the ground."

"Everything gone?" she whispered. "What will I do?" She opened and closed her mouth a few times, as though searching for words, before collapsing against his chest. "I'm a pauper. I have nothing and no one."

Declan ran a soothing hand down her back. "You know that's not true, lass. You have the O'Rourkes. We're behind you. And we'll never let you be alone." He cleared his throat, as though uncomfortable. "Unless you want to be."

She pressed into his embrace, shaking ever-so-slightly as the shock of her loss settled over her. "I don't want to be a burden. I don't want

…" She stilled when he gasped and cried out, as her hands touched his back. "Declan?"

"Don't touch my back," he rasped in a pain-laced voice. "God, 'tis like it's still on fire." He rested his head on her shoulder, as he shuddered, while trying to corral the pain.

Pushing back from his embrace, Lorena studied him, paling as she saw the sweat on his brow and the fierce concentration as he took deep breaths to marshal the strength to beat back the pain he felt. "Declan?" she whispered. "What happened?"

He opened his eyes, causing her to gasp at the agony in his gaze. "Somethin' fell on my back, while I carried you out. I ignored it, but it burned my skin." He held on to her when she attempted to scramble from his hold. "No, Lo, … Lorena, let me hold you. Just … don't touch my back."

She gripped his strong arms, tears leaking down her cheeks. "How can you be so strong and worry about me, when you're the one injured? You must go to bed and sleep."

His blue eyes shone with joy and a hint of teasing, as he looked at her. "I did sleep. And knowing you're well is the best tonic I'll ever receive." He kissed her forehead. "Come, Lorena," he murmured into her ear in his deep voice, earning a shiver. "Let me hold you a little longer, before we are disturbed."

She relaxed into his embrace, attempting to convince herself that all she felt was gratitude and friendship toward Declan. She refused to admit the depth of her lie.

CHAPTER 9

The following day, Lorena stood in front of the burned-out shell of her business, a resolute expression pasted on. Inside, she was howling and weeping and wailing at fate. Outside, she stared dully at the ruined embodiment of her dreams. She gripped her hands tightly, so that her fingernails gouged her palms, the pain preventing tears from coursing down her cheeks.

"Oh, my poor niece," Uriah Chaffee huffed out, as he stood beside her, surveying the wreckage. "How you must be so devastated to see your dreams go up in smoke." He lifted his hand, as though to indicate smoke rising in the air. "To know you will be dependent on the O'Rourkes forever."

She refused to look at him. "This is a minor setback."

He huffed out an astonished breath, as he shifted to stare at her, his ever-expanding paunch bumping into her side. "You call the loss of everything from Saint Louis a 'minor setback'?" He shook his head in stupefaction. "Seamus might be generous, but he's a businessman. He expects to earn his money back from what he invested in you."

Gasping, Lorena stared in horror at her uncle. "How do you know about that?"

"I'm a lawyer. People talk to me," he said with pride, as he hooked his thumbs through his waistcoat. "If you thought you could conceal your little agreement with the O'Rourke himself, you're a fool." He looked her over. "Although I always knew you were. You turned down workin' with your own family. And you haven't had the sense to capitalize on the value of your beauty."

"There is no money to be made off my beauty," she hissed. When he opened his mouth to protest, she hissed, "No *honorable* money."

"Well, we clearly have differing opinions on what is honorable. Earning money is earning money. And I can't imagine the O'Rourkes relish the thought of caring for you for the rest of their lives." He leaned over, speaking in a softly venomous voice, his beady eyes lit with passionate fervency. "One day you'll regret spurning me. You'll regret having no ready form of income. And all because you had your head in the clouds, before watching your dreams go up in smoke. I'll enjoy watching you crawl to me, begging for help."

He turned away, leaving Lorena quivering, as she stared at the charred remains of her store. Her mind spun with all her uncle had said and implied. Seamus had been generous in his support of her, but he was a businessman. She had known her store would be successful, even if it took her time to repay him. But how would she pay him back now? Now that she had nothing?

She ran a hand down her arm, until her hand rested on her waist. Although she knew her uncle wanted her to work in his friend's saloon, she couldn't imagine such a life. Flirting and teasing men. Taunting them while scantily clothed, as they became drunker and drunker. Why would they believe she had no interest in fulfilling what she had teased them with?

With a soft moan, she considered the Madam. Although a good friend to the O'Rourkes, Lorena had never considered Nora more than a distant acquaintance. Although the Madam had aided her injured sister Phoebe, lending Maggie herbs and books filled with medical theory, Lorena had little faith the Madam would proffer any aid, other than a bed, while Lorena worked among her girls. She shivered at the thought of working at the Bordello.

Her mind spun. What was she to do? How could she possibly pay Seamus back?

~

A few hours later, Declan stared at the blackened wreckage of the store. Rather than the pile of smoking timber and charred ground covered in ash, he saw Lorena. Helpless and unconscious. Unable to escape an inferno. His jaw tightened, as he battled back images that he feared would never fully fade from his memory.

"Are you well?" asked a woman, her voice solicitous, melodious.

Declan spun to face the attractive woman who ran the Bordello, dressed in a bright fuchsia dress with a sheen to it that made it shine even brighter. Her brown hair was pulled back in an attractive knot, and her brown eyes were filled with concern. "I'm fine, ma'am," he stammered out. "I'm afraid I've not made your acquaintance." He took a step back, as though worried he shouldn't speak with her.

"Oh, I'm friends with your family." She paused, waiting to see if he would argue with her on that point. When he continued to stand beside her, she relaxed a little. "How is Miss Mortimer? I was worried about her on the night of the fire."

Declan's stiff posture relaxed, as he belatedly recalled the Madam had come to aid Lorena. "You were there," he breathed. "I forgot. Thank you for helping her." He paused, scratching at his brow. "She's well. Tired. Devastated." He motioned to the wreckage in front of them.

"She almost lost everything," Nora murmured, in her deep husky voice. When Declan stared at her in confusion, she said in a low voice, "She's alive. And so are you. Anything remains possible." She paused, staring at him a long moment. "Mary mentioned you were injured. Are you well?"

Declan shrugged and then hissed at the motion. "I've a burn on my back. It aches a bit, but it'll heal."

"Don't be too proud," Nora admonished. "Accept the advice

Maggie offers, as she is becoming a proficient healer." After a slight pause, she murmured, "And be on your guard for her. Please."

Focusing fully on the Madam, he ignored the ache in his back. "For Maggie?" he asked. At her nod, he took a slight step closer to her and spoke in a soft voice. "Why tell me and not Da or Mum?"

Nora sighed, her gaze clouded. "Seamus has always been a good friend to me. Your mother has proven equally generous in her amity. However, I know Seamus and I can imagine a mother's fear." Her eyes glowed with a deep emotion for a moment, before any such feeling was hidden away behind a resolute facade. "I worry they would act rashly. And this situation calls for planning and strategy."

"Da's always been the best at outwittin' an opponent," Declan said, standing tall as he defended his da.

"I imagine he has. But that was business. This is about a man who is intent on stealing Maggie away." She paused and took a deep breath. "From what I've heard, if he can't steal her away, he plans to ensure no one else ever has the pleasure of her company, ever again."

Declan paled. "You mean, he'd …" He shook his head and swallowed, unable to say the words. Unable to utter the unthinkable. That his sweet sister could be so harmed.

"Yes," Nora whispered. "I know Seamus was clever enough to trick the man out of town. That was child's play for what I hear Jacques has planned. Whether it's this year or next, the man is coming back. And you all must be prepared. Talk to your father, Declan. Let him know I will be expecting his summons."

Declan nodded, watching her walk away, as his mind raced with fear.

Lorena squinted as she entered the darkened interior of the warehouse, taking a few moments to adjust from the brightness outside. Her gaze roved over the tidy shelves of supplies, waiting to be purchased, ignoring a few crates in the corner that were still to be unpacked.

Niall glanced up from reading a book, his green eyes ablaze with curiosity, as he looked at her. "Miss," he said. Although he'd always been friendly, he had never as readily accepted her into the family, as his parents and Maggie had. "What can I do for you?" He tucked a strand of black hair behind one ear, standing up and setting aside his book. Although lanky, it was evident he would become as tall and as strong as Seamus.

"I'm looking for your father."

Niall nodded his head in the direction of a doorway. "He's in his office. He won't mind an interruption." A smile teased his lips, before disappearing. "He's making a list for supplies for next year. He calls it one of Hercules's lost labors."

Lorena sputtered out a laugh, whispering her thanks, as she walked with a purposeful stride to the office doorway. She raised her hand to knock, her hand frozen in air, when she saw Seamus leaned over his desk, a hand in his hair, as he muttered to himself about impossibilities. "Mr. O'Rourke?" she called out.

"Ah, lass, how many times must I tell you to call me Seamus?" He rose, smiling broadly. "You're a sight for sore eyes, and the distraction I need."

Forcing a smile to hide her trepidation, Lorena entered his office with a feigned confidence. "I know I must speak with you. It's only fair, after all you've done for me."

"Done for you?" He tilted his head to one side and shook his head in confusion. "Come. Sit and let's discuss your odd notion." He waited until she had settled, and then he relaxed into his comfortable chair behind his desk across from her. "What's the matter, lass?"

"You're a businessman. A successful one." She gripped and ungripped her hands together. "I had hoped I too would find success." Her voice faded away, her gaze distant, as she saw the charred hull of her store.

"And you would have been, had it not been for the fire," Seamus said. "What's the matter?"

"I don't have the means to repay you. I … I don't know what to do."

She took a deep breath, biting the side of one lip, as she forced herself to meet his gaze. "I spoke with my uncle."

Seamus leaned back in his chair, the squeaking it made the only sound in the room. "Did you now? And what did you learn?"

Lorena moved her mouth, as though trying to speak, but no words came out. She looked at Seamus in a panic.

Leaning forward, Seamus stared at her with a fierce intensity. "If I were a bettin' man, I'd bet everythin' I own that he tried to convince you to join him in his worthless endeavor with Bell. To become a Temptress."

Shrugging, she whispered, "Not in so many words."

"Nay, but he implied it." He rose, pacing behind his desk. "Did he talk about my wonderful business ventures an' that a man like me must always be paid back?" At her nod, Seamus leaned forward, resting his hands on his desk as he stared at her. "What type of man am I, lass?"

"I don't understand," she whispered.

"When your uncle says, *a man like me*, what do you imagine?" He waited, as she paled and then flushed. "Do you think of me, sittin' around the family table with wee Maura, Cillian, or Gavin on my lap? Do you think of me with my Mary in my arms or laughin' at somethin' the lads said? Or is it that I'm a moneygrubbin' Irishman who'll do anythin' for a dollar?"

"Sir—Seamus—that's not what I meant." She rubbed at her head. "I'm so confused!" She cried, tears pouring down her cheek. "I've lost everything! Everything I ever dreamed about is gone. Gone up in flames. All I have is a pile of ash." She stared at him with abject desolation. "I can't depend on your family forever."

Seamus walked around the desk to crouch in front of her, holding her hands and squeezing them. "How, after all this time, can't you understand that you're family, Lorena? You're family to me. If the café had burned to the ground, do you think I'd be after Deirdre and Ardan for repayment?" He shook his head, his gaze filled with disappointment and sadness. "'Tisn't family. 'Tisn't love."

A sob burst forth, as she fell forward into his arms.

"Ah, lass, come now," he murmured, as he held her. His hands patted at her back, as he waited for her sobs to quiet. When she had quieted to snuffling breaths against his chest, he eased her away, pulling a handkerchief from his pocket. "There's no shame in showin' your sorrow at all you've lost. Just as there's no need worryin' about rebuildin.'" He met her shocked gaze, swiping at a tear that trickled down her cheek, as though she were Maggie or Niamh and needing his care.

"I could never," she whispered. "How would I ever repay you?"

Seamus let out a deep breath. "Lorena, would you cease with the talk of repayment?" He looked at her with a quiet solemnity. "Come. Let me help you up." He eased her to standing, stepping away from her, as she had curled into herself at his nearness. "All will be well, lass." He paused. "As long as you never believe the lies told you by your uncle."

She met his gaze, standing a bit taller. "I won't. He's a snake." She whispered her thanks before slipping from the room, unseeingly fleeing the warehouse until she was outside and headed toward home. She prayed Winnifred was away, for Lorena needed time alone to think.

∼

Declan poked his head into his father's office, frowning when he saw his dad staring out the window. "Da?" he asked, as he entered and shut the door behind him. "What was Lorena doing here? Niall said he heard her crying."

Seamus heaved out a breath, turning to face his son. "She was. She has everythin' jumbled up in her mind and doesn't know up from down."

Declan shook his head and moved to race after Lorena, only stilling his instinctual movement when his father called out to him to remain. "Da?"

"Stay, son," Seamus said. "Give her a little time. She doesn't need to feel hemmed in by O'Rourkes. She already lives with us." He sobered and sat in the chair behind his desk, nodding with satisfaction as Declan sat in front of him. "She's confused, Declan. Believes she must find a way to repay her debt to me."

Declan sat back, grimacing, as he forgot about his injury and sat with too much force against his healing scar. "I can see why she would be worried, but she must know by now that's now how we are." He paused when his father stared at him, as though waiting for him to fit together pieces of a puzzle. "Has her uncle spoken with her lately?" He canted forward, his fingers tapping an irritated tattoo on his father's desktop.

Seamus smiled with pleasure at his son's astuteness. "Aye. Just this mornin' Chaffee spoke with the lass. Believes he can influence her, now that she's destitute."

Swearing under his breath, Declan bowed his head forward. "That's all she needed to hear. She was already worried about being a pauper. Worried we'd see her as a burden." He stared at his father.

Leaning back in his chair, Seamus studied his son. "What do you want to do, my lad?"

Shrugging, Declan stared out the side window. "I don't know. I care for her, Da. I won't lie." He closed his eyes. "And my heart feels as though burstin' at the sight of her carin' for wee Gavin." He looked at his father with fathomless emotions in his gaze. "But I ... 'Tis too soon."

A long silence ensued, where the quiet conversation of Niall and Kevin trickled in from the warehouse. Seamus shifted again in his chair. "What are you to do, my boy?" He waited, as Declan stared at him. "You've taken little interest in workin' in the warehouse again, and now the bookstore's burned to the ground."

Declan nodded. Taking a long breath, he whispered, "How many children live in town?"

A proud glint filled Seamus's gaze. "At most, a few dozen."

"Would the town pay for a teacher?" he whispered, staring at his father with nascent hope. "I ... I believe I'd be good at it, Da."

Smiling, Seamus nodded. "Aye, you would. But there's the matter of fundin' a school. And convincing the townsfolk that 'tis worth sendin' children to school."

"You always ensured we had some schooling, teaching us all you could," Declan said. "You instilled a desire to always learn more."

"In you, perhaps," Seamus said, with a wry chuckle. "You were always the most curious and always wanted to read more and more." He sighed. "I did what I could, lad, but I know you could have learned more, had you had proper schooling."

After a long moment of silence, Seamus mused, "You wouldn't have a school year-round, and the wages would be meager. But if you had a school *and* a bookstore …" Seamus lifted a brow, as he tossed a paperweight from palm to palm, while he studied his son. "That could be a fine business. Perhaps begin as a tutor to a few of the children in town, while we allow the idea of a school to bloom. Sometimes these things must take root to flourish."

Flushing, Declan rubbed at the back of his neck. "Now you're assumin' I'll formalize my association with Lorena."

Seamus's eyes twinkled with mischief. "And why shouldn't you, Dec?" He sobered when he saw his son fidget across from him. "Declan, is there somethin' more botherin' you?"

"Aye," Declan murmured. "I should have said something after I spoke with A.J., when Winnifred slapped Lorena. But I was too focused on Lorena. I can't allow my concern for Lorena to distract me from the threat to Maggie."

"Maggie," Seamus breathed, leaning forward. "What threat?" He cocked his head to one side, as his muscles coiled and bunched, ready to strike at a hidden adversary at any moment.

Nodding, Declan spoke in a soft voice. "Both A.J. and the Madam have told me that they've heard rumblings that Jacques is plannin' to return." He clenched his jaw a moment before rasping, "A.J. had heard the weasel planned to steal her away." At Seamus's growl of displeasure, Declan shook his head. "Nay, Da, 'tis worse than that."

"Worse?" Seamus hissed. "How can anythin' be worse than havin' our wee Maggie stolen from us?" He paled when he saw the desperation and fear in his son's gaze. "He wouldn't," he breathed.

"Aye," Declan whispered. "The Madam said she heard that, if he can't steal her away, he'd ensure no one else ever had the pleasure of her company."

"He'd kill my wee babe?" Seamus asked. Slamming his hands on his desk, he rose to his full height, his eyes gleaming with defiance and determination. "Nay, he'll never have the chance." Taking a deep breath, he looked to Declan. "Dunmore said Jacques is in a mining town, near Cataract Creek." At Declan's curious stare, he muttered, "A fair distance from Helena but not as far as Virginia City."

"He could leave there at any moment, Da. Return here."

"Aye," Seamus murmured. "We've always known that to be true. I'd hoped his fascination with Maggie had waned during the past two years." He sighed and lowered his head to his hands, as he sat down. "How am I to tell your mum? Tell Maggie?"

Declan rubbed a thumb over his jaw, as he listened to Niall whistling. "Wait until Dunmore's back. Then we should have a meeting. With him and A.J. and the Madam."

Seamus nodded. "Aye. We have to prepare. For no one threatens our family."

~

Declan walked to the edge of the small stream that fed into the Missouri. This had been the O'Rourke thinking spot since they had arrived in town, even when the stream was little more than a trickle. Today, a small amount of water tumbled over rocks, causing a soothing lullaby sound. He attempted to focus on nature. On the birds flitting from branch to branch. On anything other than Lorena. However, that proved impossible.

His arms ached from the memory of holding her and yearned to hold her again. His face craved the sensation of her silky hair teasing and tickling his skin again, while breathing in the subtle scents of roses mixed with soap. Unbidden, he longed for the sense of peace he had felt with her.

Although he had just met her a month ago, he felt like he had known her much longer. As though they had met in another time and were now finally deepening their friendship. He battled back resentment that he had not met her in Saint Louis before she departed for Fort Benton. That he had somehow been spared the heartbreak of Magnolia, yet not the love of Gavin. He shook his head at his roiling thoughts. For if he had met Lorena rather than Magnolia, how very different would his life be now?

He closed his eyes, the comforting sound of the creek blocking out everything else around him, and he envisioned what he could have. A home with a woman whose eyes lit up at the sight of him. A home where there was laughter, passion, and respect. Where the comfort and joy he felt in her store was a daily part of his life. He sighed.

He thought about his conversation with his father. Why shouldn't he formalize his association with the woman who fascinated him? He took a deep stuttering breath as he admitted he was terrified of suffering again. Of experiencing a far deeper pain than anything he'd felt with Magnolia. For this time he knew and liked Lorena. She wasn't a dream he'd fabricated. With a groan, he rubbed at his forehead.

"What bothers you, Declan?"

He spun, blinking a few times, as he stared at Lorena standing behind him in a simple light-green dress that highlighted the brilliance of her red hair and enhanced the green of her eyes. "Lorena," he breathed, as though he had conjured her.

"Yes," she said with a wry smile. "Are you well?"

He cleared his throat and shrugged, pointing toward the creek. "I was enjoying the day."

"You looked as though you were having a waking dream, as your father would say." She flushed when he stared at her intently. "I don't mean to pry."

"Are you well, lass?" His gaze roved over her, as though searching for concealed injuries.

She lifted and lowered her shoulders, her arms wrapped around herself in a protective manner. "I'm well. As well as can be expected now that my business is ..." She bit off the bitter words that threatened to spill out. "None of that." She turned to face him with a brilliant smile that did little to conceal the desperation, fear, and despair enveloping her. "I've a proposition."

He stilled, his muscles tightening in foreboding. "Proposition?"

She smiled brightly, as though she had come up with the most brilliant plan. "Yes." She swiped a hand down her skirts and then met his gaze again. "I know I don't have much to offer, but I ... I'm good with Gavin, and we have interesting conversations. I'm a decent cook, and I can sew a straight line. And I think you and I are friends."

Declan frowned at her portrayal of herself. "Aye?" He tilted his head to one side, as he studied her. "All that you say is true, except the part about you not having much to offer."

She rolled her eyes at him and huffed out a breath. "Marry me, Declan. Let me be your wife."

"What?" He scratched at his head and backed up a step, nearly tumbling backward into the creek. Lorena reached forward, gripping his arm and tugging him forward. They stumbled and tumbled to the ground, him landing beside her. "Ouch," he muttered as he landed awkwardly, so as not to crush her, pulling the healing scar on his back, feeling as though it had torn open.

She rested beside him, her eyes closed, her face the perfect picture of absolute misery, although no tears fell. She did not lean in to him or attempt to garner any comfort from his nearness. "I'm sorry. All I do is cause pain."

"Lo," he whispered, "you know that's not true." He paused, waiting for her reply. When she remained quiet, he asked, "Why aren't you crying an' keenin' an' screamin' at fate for what's occurred? Why are you so composed?"

"Nothing ever comes from strong emotions," she whispered. "Except a headache and regret."

He chuckled, smiling at her tenderly when she opened her eyes to glare at him. His fingers played over her jaw. "Nay," he continued in a soft voice. "They help. They prove we are alive. That we aren't afraid to be among the livin'." His eyes clouded. "No matter how much you wish otherwise, love, you feel. We all feel." He paused and shook his head, his gaze now sorrowful. "I will not be used to improve your opinion of yourself."

"No!" she gasped, reaching forward to hold his arm and to prevent him from rising. "That's not it at all. I … I owe your father—" She broke off with a gasp, when he pushed up and strode away a few paces, swearing under his breath. "*That's* not it at all," she pleaded, tears now leaking out. "Please, listen."

"What is it, Lorena?" he asked in a defeated voice, his head bowed, as he stared away from her toward town. "That you want to marry me out of desperation? Pity? Duty?" He looked back at her with his eyes ablaze. "Is there any feelin' in you at all?"

She abruptly pushed herself up, striding to him with her skirts whipping around her ankles. "Of course there is!" she snapped. "But I don't want to feel! I never want to feel again!" She held a hand to her mouth, as her eyes rounded in shock at her admission. "Declan, please."

"So you'd trap me in a loveless marriage, just so I'd have a woman to play mother to wee Gavin?" he murmured. "How can you not understand I want so much more than that?" When she took a step toward him, he backed away. "Nay, Lorena. Leave me be to think." He spun on his heel and strode toward town.

"Ah, sonny, it seems your woman has you tied up in knots," A.J. said, as he settled on a crate beside Declan a few hours later. He sat, staring out at the timeless flow of the Missouri and the cliffs on the other side of the river. The sun shone on them, and they glowed a rich sandy yellow.

"She's not my woman," Declan said sullenly.

Laughing, A.J. tapped his knee. "Well, if she ain't yours, she ain't no one else's. She's as prickly as a porcupine, except for when she's with you. Can't see her takin' a shine to another anytime soon." He looked at Declan. "When's the last time you chatted until you were *hearse?*"

"I ain't dead," Declan muttered, before huffing out a laugh. "*Hoarse.*

And I was never hoarse with her. We chatted, aye, but it wasn't anything remarkable."

A.J. sat working on his pipe, before taking a long pull on it. "Nothin' remarkable, sonny?" he asked with an incredulous lift of one eyebrow. "You chattered away with her for hours on end about every topic known to man. An' she matched your wits an' your curiosity. Tell me when you've found another woman who's managed to do that."

Declan glared at A.J. "She feels guilty about the store. She sees marryin' me as a way to ease the debt owed my father."

A long silence ensued, where A.J. sat muttering to himself, as his jaw intermittently clamped down on his pipe. Finally he said, "Did you ever consider that's what she tells herself, so she ain't so afraid at her desire to wed you?" A.J.'s dark-brown eyes glowed with frank intelligence, as he met Declan's gaze.

"What have I ever done to scare her?"

Huffing out a snort of laughter, A.J. slapped his hand against his leg. "Oh, sonny, you don't understand women at all. I barely understand 'em, but you're a babe in the manger, as the preacher would say." He sighed, as he scratched at his head. "It's obvious to anyone who looks that she lost someone she loved. Why wouldn't she be afraid of losin' you too?" A.J. shrugged.

"How is it obvious?" Declan asked.

"Hidin' her life away in books. Keepin' herself apart, even when she's in a horde of O'Rourkes. Never believin' your parents' acceptance of her into your family." A.J. puffed on his pipe, watching white pelicans swoop and soar over the Missouri. "I know it might feel that way, sonny, but you don't have a monopoly on heartache."

Declan heaved out a breath, his shoulders slouched over. "I don't want to be used. Not again."

"Well, I'd be tellin' her that, not me," the older man said, as he stood, slapping Declan on his shoulder. "Last I saw, she was headin' into your brother's café."

Declan nodded his thanks, spending a few more moments in quiet contemplation, before rising to walk to the café. Rather than enter the front and have to visit with the patrons, he circled around back. He paused on the top step, closing his eyes, as he listened to two women singing in perfect harmony.

Poking his head around the side of the door, he saw Deirdre—standing with her eyes closed, her hands submerged in a bowl of dough as she sang—while Lorena stood at the sink, scrubbing a pot, her voice the perfect counterpoint to Deirdre's. When they finished, Declan blurted out, "What are you doing here?"

Lorena spun to face him, her eyes widening in shock. "Deirdre needed help, and I have little to occupy my time right now." She shrugged and turned back to the sink.

He shot a quick glance in his sister-in-law's direction, ignoring her curious smile. "Lorena, I need to speak with you. Can the dishes wait a few more minutes, Deirdre?" At Deirdre's softly murmured assent, Lorena hissed out her discontent, before following Declan outside.

When he moved in the direction of the stream, she stopped, her hands on her hips. "Why are we returning there?"

He faced her, motioning for her to join him. When she stood beside him, he walked at a slower pace, so they could walk together. "I want privacy, and few venture to the stream."

After they arrived, he stared into the tumbling water for so long that she huffed out an aggrieved breath. "I'll return to help Deirdre."

"No!" Declan grabbed her hand. "No. We need to talk." He looked deeply into her eyes that were more guarded than he'd ever seen them. "You don't trust me anymore," he breathed.

She pushed at his chest, propelling him back a step. "You don't want me!"

Smiling, he reached out a hand to caress her cheek, before dropping it and standing solemnly in front of her. "'Tisn't true." He made a conciliatory gesture. "Not entirely true." He waited for her to calm, as he gazed into her beautiful eyes. "I don't want you if you're acting out of guilt or a sense of indebtedness to my family. I don't want you if, … if you feel nothing for *me*." His eyes shone with his sincerity and the hope he could not hide.

She gaped at him, unconsciously taking a step toward him.

"Declan, I never meant ..." She broke off what more she would have said before whispering, "I never meant to make you feel superfluous. I never thought to meet a man like you. A man who could be a true friend." She had looked down, missing his wince at her calling him *a friend*. "I always thought I'd go through life alone."

"Well, then, lass, your first proposal was a bit shabby. Would you care to try to improve it?" He grinned, as she giggled at his teasing.

She paused for a long moment, gathering her thoughts, before taking a deep breath. She let it out, as she firmed her shoulders, meeting his hopeful gave. "Declan O'Rourke, I'm terrified of feeling again." She faltered as she looked into his penetrating gaze. "But I realize I already do," she admitted on a soft whisper. "I care for you and Gavin." She reached forward, when he shifted with unease. "I don't speak because I only want Gavin in my life. How can you doubt my sincerity after all our conversations? All the laughter we've shared?" She waited until she saw him nod in understanding. "There are things I must tell you but not yet."

"Aye, Lo," he said in a low voice, "as there is much you don't yet understand about me."

"When I learned you'd been injured, saving me from the fire ..." Her voice broke off, and she blinked away tears. "I never considered myself worthy of such concern."

"Ah, lass," he rasped, as he took a step forward, and cupped her jaw with one of his large hands. "You know you are. To me."

"So I'm learning," she whispered, as she moved her face, so his fingers slid over her cheek. "I won't promise to be a good wife. I know I'll disappoint you. But I'm loyal and true."

"Will you pine for another while you are with me?" he asked.

She stared at him with shadows and fears in her gaze. "I pine for no living man."

Declan paused, taking a deep breath, as he thought through her answer. Finally he smiled and nodded.

Lorena frowned, uncertain what he was waiting for. Finally she blurted out, "Will you marry me?"

A huge smile burst forth, and he chuckled. "I thought you'd never ask. Of course I'll marry you, Lo." He swooped forward, kissing her softly, before deepening the kiss. He hauled her close, holding her pressed against his chest, as his fingers dug into her hair and back. "We'll be happy. I promise."

She gripped his arms, careful not to hurt his healing wound, and pressed her face against his chest. "Yes," she whispered, praying their vow would make it true.

CHAPTER 10

Two weeks later, Declan sat in the room he shared with Eamon, listening to the excited chatter of his younger brothers in their nearby bedroom and the gentle hum of his sisters' voices downstairs. He strained for any sign of Lorena, but he knew she was at Phoebe's, preparing for their wedding. He glanced out the window, relieved to see the beauty of another Montana summer day.

"Are you about done preenin' at yourself in the mirror?" Ardan asked, as he stepped inside. He wore his best suit, and he'd tied back his shoulder-length hair. Although he teased his younger brother, he was unable to hide a hint of concern in his gaze.

Declan glared at him and then smiled. "I'm not preenin'." He laughed. "I wish I'd been here to tease you when you wed your Deirdre."

"Well, 'tis what brothers do." He looked long and hard at Declan. "You're sure?" When Declan stared at him with a mixture of hope and trepidation, he closed his eyes. "'Twill all work out, Dec. She's a good woman. Nothin' like her youngest sister."

"Aye," he whispered. "She is not." After a moment, he took a deep breath. "I won't abandon her at the altar. I want a wife. And a mother for Gavin."

Ardan strode to him, gripping his shoulder, his eyes lit with a fervent intensity. "You deserve someone to love you, Dec, to the depths of your soul."

Declan shrugged, as he stared at his eldest brother. "I don't know if I inspire such sentiment, Ardan." He let out a deep breath and whispered, "She promised she doesn't yearn for a living man."

"Feck," Ardan rasped. "Which means she could pine for a ghost." He met his brother's gaze, equally haunted with impotent worry. "How do you fight a ghost?"

Shaking his head, Declan smiled sadly. He slipped on his best suit coat, fingering the red waistcoat and the ring held within the pocket over his heart. "I don't know. 'Tis disconcerting to realize I'm a Colleen." He closed his eyes, as he attempted to rid himself of the miserable memories of his childhood, after their mum had been lost to them and their father had married Colleen. A basically good woman, she had always desired what their da couldn't give her—the depth of love he had only ever felt for Mary.

"You are so much more than that. You shouldn't marry her if you have such doubts," Ardan protested.

Declan scoffed, running a hand through his trimmed hair and then over his trimmed beard. "Tell me, Ardan, who am I to marry then? Every woman I've ever been interested in has chosen another. I know Lorena wants to marry me because she asked me." He flushed at admitting that fact to his brother.

Ardan nodded, jerking when he heard Da calling for them. "Be happy, brother. Find joy with her. And be brave enough to demand happiness."

Declan took one more deep breath, before following his brother out of the room and to the wedding site in a field away from town.

That evening, Lorena stood by the bed in the hotel room Declan had rented for them. She attempted to ignore shouts from the men in the saloon and the voices of men carousing outside, as they searched out their nightly entertainment. As the door opened to their room, she spun with a gasp, her eyes widening with fear. At the sight of Declan entering, she heaved out a breath and attempted a weak smile.

"Are you well, love?" he asked, as he closed and latched the door. "I thought you'd want time to freshen up." He motioned at her and then to the basin of fresh water nearby.

"Oh," she whispered in a defeated voice. Fingering the fine embroidery of the moss-green dress she wore, she gazed at him in confusion. "I had thought you'd help me from my dress. It is our wedding night."

He flushed and nodded. "Of course." He took a purposeful step toward her, freezing when he saw her stiffen at his approach. "Lo?"

"I … I shouldn't be so skittish," she whispered. "It's not as though …" She shook her head and forced a bright smile. "I trust you, Declan."

He stared at her for a long moment, before pulling a chair closer to where she stood. He settled in it, giving every appearance of having no care in the world. "Do you?" he murmured. "What have I done to earn it?"

She sat on the bed, her momentary trepidation disappearing, as they began to converse. "You've always treated me with respect. You listen to me and don't judge me for having opinions that don't agree with yours." She smiled as she saw the shared remembrance of their conversations in his gaze. "You ensured I was well, when no one else would have sought me out."

"I don't want you to idolize me for doing what was right, Lo," he muttered with a shake of his head.

When she touched his hand, his gaze met hers. "I don't, but I wish you would allow me to appreciate what you did. Few would have cared," she whispered. "And none would have sat by my bed and then held me as I mourned, easing my fears." She smiled at him. "You're a good man, Declan O'Rourke." She took a deep breath, her cheeks a rosy pink. "When I saw you waiting for me at the end of the altar, I couldn't believe such a man wanted to marry me. Would agree to marry me." Her gaze was filled with wonder.

He leaned forward, pressing his forehead against hers and wrapping his arms around her waist. "Why doubt, Lo? You're remarkable and brave and beautiful. I thought my heart would stop when I saw you in this gorgeous dress that only made your hair even more glorious and your eyes shine brighter. I couldn't believe you wanted *me*."

She ran one hand through his hair, as the palm of her other hand scraped over his trimmed beard. "Of course I did. Only a fool wouldn't want you, Declan." She gasped as he tugged her into his arms, kissing her passionately. She gasped again when he lay her on the bed, coming to lay atop her.

Arching up into his touch, she chased his fleeting caresses, each stroke of his hand too short to bring any relief to the fire she felt burning through her body. "Declan, please," she gasped, as she kissed along his jaw. "Please, teach me. I don't know how to please you, but I want to."

He pushed away, his lips moving down her long neck. "Never doubt how much you please me, Lo." He kissed the underside of her jaw. "Yes, my Lorena, I'll love you," he whispered, his words provoking a shiver. "Let me," he murmured, as he urged her to her side and unbuttoned her dress, kissing his way down her back.

After helping her up to shuck her dress and undergarments, he stripped off his clothes and joined her under the covers. When she would have restarted their wild, passionate caresses, he urged her to rest against him a moment, accustoming herself to the feel of him. Only when he felt her relax did he begin to caress and kiss her again. "Is this all right?" he whispered, as he kissed her shoulder.

"Show me," she gasped, as she ran her hands over his back.

"Never doubt how much I adore you," he murmured, before he deepened the kiss, and they were lost to words.

Declan sat in a chair beside his marriage bed, watching his bride sleep. Her red hair spilled over the pillow, and his fingers itched to run through the silky strands. Her milk-white skin with a smattering of freckles shone in the faint lamplight, as though teasing him to lean forward and to kiss his way to her neck. However, he remained seated, lost in thought.

Finally he was a married man. Finally Gavin would have a woman who would be his mum. Declan waited for the deep contentment to fill him. For an overwhelming sense of accomplishment. For an unmistakable pride that he had finally matched his brothers.

Instead a deep ache, akin to sorrow, permeated his soul. Rather than a marriage founded on love, his was founded on deception. On half-truths. And a barely established friendship. For he now knew she didn't trust him. And he'd had no illusion she had loved him when they married.

Like a fool, he'd hoped she would come to love him. That she would come to desire him, so his marriage would rival the joyous unions shared by his brothers. Instead she had deceived him. Had called him *Josiah*, just before she had slipped into sleep.

With a profound sorrow, as he mourned what could have been, he watched her sleep, knowing their time of reckoning approached.

~

Lorena woke the following morning with a deep sense of contentment. She rolled over, stilling as she realized she was naked under the sheets. With a gasp, she pulled the sheets to her nose and looked around the room, paling when she saw Declan, fully dressed, sitting in a chair beside the bed, staring at her. "Declan? Why aren't you in bed with me?"

"I think better out of bed."

"Think?" she asked, scooting up to a sitting position, holding the sheet at her jaw. "Why would you need to think on our wedding night?" She squirmed as he stared at her long and hard, his jaw tightening, as though with anger, while he contemplated her.

"Are you upset I slept so much?" she asked. "I'm sorry. I didn't sleep the night before our wedding. I was nervous. And then, … after, I couldn't help but fall asleep. You should have woken me. I would have

…" Her voice trailed away, as he continued to stare at her with unveiled disappointment. "What did I do?" she asked in a low voice, her shoulders hunching up around her to protect herself.

"It's what you didn't do," Declan said.

"I told you that I didn't know how to please a man! I didn't know what I was doing!" she protested, as tears coursed down her cheeks.

Declan shook his head. "How can you be upset with me right now? You're the one who played me false!"

Lorena gaped at him, her eyes rounded, as she thought through his words. When he nodded, she swallowed. "I wasn't sure you could tell." She bit her lip at the inanity of the comment.

"Tell that I wasn't your first lover?" he asked. "Or tell that you didn't trust me enough to tell me before we tumbled into bed?" He paused as she remained quiet, her gaze lowered. "Or the fact you've had a child?" He nodded, as her horrified gaze shot up to meet his.

"How?" she gasped. "How could you possibly know that?"

"A wild guess. One you've only just proven. So where is your child? Should I expect him or her any day now? Add to my family so I have a little menagerie of bastards?" He gasped as her hand connected to his cheek, the slap sounding through the room.

"Don't ever speak about Gavin in such a way. Or my baby," she said, as a keening wail escaped. "Never. They deserve better."

Declan rose. "It appears we all deserve better."

She watched with horror as he strode from their hotel room, slamming the door behind him.

Declan settled into the Sunrise Saloon, eager for a drink and to be left alone. He hoped none of his brothers would be here, and he suspected most would be at work or with the family. He motioned for the barkeep, Stanley Robinson, to give him a shot of firewater. After slugging it back in one swallow, he hissed for another. After swallowing it down too, he stood, staring into space, as, unbidden, a memory resurfaced.

The thick scent of her cloying perfume wafted over him, as he watched her stuff dresses, petticoats, and undergarments into a trunk. "What are you doing, Magnolia?" he asked. "Our ship doesn't leave for a few more weeks."

She strolled toward him with a practiced sway to her hips, smiling with satisfaction as she saw him instinctively follow her movement with his gaze. "Your ship, you mean." She stopped just in front of him, raising a manicured finger to trace over his jaw and then down his chest. "You're a fool, Declan. But then, what else should I have expected from an Irishman?"

Her cackle caused the hair on the back of his neck to rise, and he bit back his protest that he wasn't a fool. Looking at her, seeing her disdain, he felt like one. "So you're not coming with me."

"Ah, the simpleton finally understands!" she said with sarcastic glee. "No, I'm not joining you in that tiny worthless trading town in the middle of nowhere." She held her hands on her hips, covered in ice-blue satin. "Do you believe one such as I should waste myself in such a place?" She rolled her eyes as she strolled away, her pleasure dimming when she noted that Declan wasn't as enthralled by her feminine antics as before.

"Where are you going?" he asked.

"Who's to say I'm going anywhere?" she asked.

He waved at her trunk and waited. "You may call me a fool, but I know a woman desperate to leave."

She smiled at him. "You are a fool and gullible and naive." She approached him again, pressing his hand against her belly. "But I do thank you for giving me what I wanted." She cackled with glee when he paled. "Enjoy your worthless family. You believe you'll find a woman to love you, but you're too much of a dimwit to understand no woman could ever love you. How could she? You're not nearly as attractive as your brothers, and you're boring." She raised a bell, and a large servant appeared, ushering Declan from the room.

"This isn't the end, Magnolia!" he cried out, as her door slammed in his face.

The sound of a glass striking the wooden bar brought him back to the present, and he stared with a lost gaze at the barkeep. He accepted the drink but didn't raise it to his lips. He shook his head and hated that he had been such a half-wit as to follow Magnolia and to ever believe her lies that the child she carried was his. With a long exhale, he closed his eyes again and swore on all he held holy that he would never regret Gavin. A promise he knew he'd have no trouble keeping.

"Never thought to find you here today, sonny," A.J. said, as he sidled up to him.

"What are you doing here, Captain?" Declan asked. "Isn't there someone else you can pester?"

"*Hmm*, pester. Now that's what a wife's good for." A.J. looked around. "Seems you've lost yours already. Damn shame, considerin' you've been married only a day." A.J. raised his eyebrows up and down, as though to indicate Declan was a dunce to be in a saloon rather than with his wife. "Now what'd that beautiful bride of yours do to turn you so mulish?"

"I'm not mulish," Declan growled, before tossing back the next shot. He hissed at the burn down his throat. "I have every right to be bitter."

A.J. slapped him on his shoulder and pushed him to a quiet corner. "Too many folks interested in you O'Rourkes. Like you're celebrities in this town. Now what happened?"

Declan stared into the older man's eyes and shook his head. "I'm not discussin' my weddin' night with you." He swore as his words were slightly slurred. "I should know better than to drink that rotgut."

"Aye, you should, sonny. Especially considerin' your father has some of the finest whiskey in the Territory." A.J. paused a moment. "Did ye realize ye weren't the first man to discover your wife's charms?"

Gaping at the man slightly older than Ardan, Declan stared at him in wonder.

"I've struck the magpie dumb," A.J. said with pride. "I've heard all about you chatterin' away to your missus. Made me realize I hadn't been wrong when I thought she was the woman for you. No man talks and talks to a woman he doesn't want to impress."

"You're wrong, A.J. She played me for a fool. Just like Magnolia did."

A.J. huffed out a breath and crossed his arms over his chest.

"Never did meet that Magnolia woman but seems like she did a number on you. She must have been a beautiful woman, for how attractive your boy is. Now most pretty women find their beauty a curse, not a blessing. For that's all they're known for. Not their good nature or ability to help others heal. Not their fine cookin' or their ability to soothe a man's soul. Only what they look like." A.J. scratched his head. "I know I'd sure hate to only be seen as an ornament."

Declan stared at him in confusion. "My wife is beautiful, A.J., but she isn't an ornament."

"How long did it take for you to notice her beauty? Five seconds? Ten?" He paused. "How long did it take for you to realize she was brilliant and could match your brains?" He nodded as he saw Declan flush with embarrassment. "A week? Two?" A.J. shrugged. "Most never even notice she's smart. All they see is a pretty figure and a comely face. You at least saw below the surface."

"That doesn't mean she didn't play me false," Declan protested.

Nodding, A.J. pursed his lips and sighed. "I suppose that means you told her all about this Magnolia woman? And your fears about your son? And your concern about your family?" When Declan stared at him as though he were crazy, A.J. nodded. "Seems you expected trust when you extended her nothing more than a grudging friendship, Declan. Marriage, and harmony in that imperfect union, doesn't work that way."

"*Imperfect union?*" Declan murmured.

"Aye, heard someone say that somewhere. Think they were talkin' about the states and the War that raged between 'em. Somehow it always made me think of marriage. Too often I see young whippersnappers thinkin' marriage will be easy." He laughed and shook his head, as though he'd just heard the best joke. "Ha. Marriage is far from easy."

Glaring at the man, Declan asked, "Then why'd you encourage me to wed?"

"Because bein' alone is worse. As you should know, sonny." He waited until Declan reluctantly nodded his agreement. "An', when you find a good woman, you should have the sense to not let her slip away."

Staring into space, contemplating his friend's words, Declan murmured, "I fear she's not a good woman. I fear I'm a fool again."

"That's your problem, sonny. You focus too much on fear. On doubt. Rather on what is." He gave Declan's shoulder a soft punch before squeezing it. "Did you pause in all your *gorified* anger to ask her about her past? About *her* fears?"

"It's not *glorified*," Declan protested, a moment before snapping his mouth shut, as A.J. glared at him. "Of course I didn't. I stormed away."

"Then you ain't different from all the people who've hurt her in the past. And that's a damn shame. And a terrible thing for her to discover on the first day of her marriage." A.J. released his shoulder and sauntered away.

CHAPTER 11

Hours later, Lorena laid on her side, staring at the hotel wall, as the sounds of the town echoed outside. Men hollering to each other. Shots firing into the air. Hoots. Whistles. Horses whinnying. Never before had she realized how grating the sounds of this town were. Of all towns were. They all had to do with man attempting to tame a place. Or a people.

With a huff, she sat up and scrubbed at her face. The first day of her marriage might be considered an unmitigated disaster. Determination thrummed through her to cease acting like a victim; Lorena stood and hastily washed before pulling on clothes. She tied her hair back in a quick braid and slipped from the room, down the stairs, and out the front, without the snoozing proprietor, Mr. Foster, noticing her departure.

Although she resented returning to the O'Rourkes as a failure, she knew she had no alternative. Now that her store was a pile of ashes, she couldn't even create a makeshift pallet there. Shivering at the thought of sleeping in a place without the protection of at least one O'Rourke, she walked down the boardwalk with the intention of returning to the big O'Rourke home.

A hand grabbed her arm, and she stifled a gasp at the impertinence. "Unhand me!" she demanded, glaring into her uncle's eyes. "You've already done enough."

"I've not done enough, if you were so addle-minded as to marry an O'Rourke," Uriah snapped. "How could you do such a thing to me, girl? You were meant to return to me, along with Winnifred. With the two of you, I would have made a fortune."

Lorena kicked at his ankle, smiling with pleasure when he grunted in pain. "I am an O'Rourke now too, and I know they will be displeased at your treatment of me." She rubbed at her arm. "You should know better by now, Uncle."

"I'm a lawyer. They're peddlers. What could they possibly do to me?" Uriah said. His inquisitive inspection of her made her squirm. "You don't have the look of a well-loved woman. In fact, I could argue that you weren't loved at all!"

Lorena stomped her foot, glaring at her uncle and the men loitering nearby, blatantly listening in on their conversation. "Cease your nonsense. I am well and truly married, uncle. Leave me be." She pushed past him.

"You'll rue the day you defied me," he called out after her.

Lorena fought tears. "I rue the day I voted to come to this town." She picked up her skirts and her pace, nearly trotting the rest of the distance to the one place that had been home to her since she had arrived. When she stumbled into the kitchen, she flushed and then burst into tears as Mary and Maggie gaped at her in concern. "I ... Forgive me for intruding."

"Intruding?" Mary said, as she eased her into her arms. "You're my daughter now. You're never intruding."

"I ... I need a place to stay. I can't remain at that horrible hotel. And Declan despises me." Lorena sobbed into Mary's shoulder, as she was eased onto the bench by the kitchen table. "I've made a mess of everything, and nothing will make it right."

Mary made soothing noises and smiled gently. "Whenever I hear someone say that, I know things will turn right again. For nothing can stay terrible forever. Just as nothing can stay wonderful forever. Remember that, love." She smiled at Maggie, as Maggie set out a cup of tea. "Now have a cup, and tell us what you want. Or tell us nothing at all. Sometimes the greatest solace can be found in silence."

Lorena sat in a dazed stupor as Mary and Maggie continued to bustle around her. Sipping her tea, a small amount of her misery eased, although she knew it wouldn't fully abate until she had made her peace with Declan. However, she didn't know how she would ever explain everything to him. With a sigh, she closed her eyes, as she envisioned telling him her most painful secrets.

"Nothing is ever as bad as you believe it is. Nor is it rarely as good as you imagine," Mary murmured, as she sat beside the younger woman. When Lorena opened her eyes, Mary smiled with kind encouragement and squeezed her hand. "You'll find your way, lass. You and Declan will."

"I don't know how we will," Lorena whispered. "I proved I don't trust him."

Mary nodded again and took another sip of her tea. "Aye, I imagine that 'tis true enough. But has he proven the same to you?" She waited. "I know my son." She shrugged as though embarrassed by her pronouncement. "Or I like to think I do. I've spent too much time apart from him to know him as well as I'd like." Her hazel eyes shone, as she spoke with a mixture of regret and hope. "Don't let him brood too long."

"I can't force him to tell me about his past."

"Nay, just as he can't force you to share more about yourself than you wish." Mary paused. "But you leaving the hotel and abandonin' him so soon after your wedding will force him to confront his worst fears."

"I have to go back?" Lorena asked in a defeated voice, her shoulders stooped.

"Nay. The hotel's no place for my son and daughter-in-law. Come with me." She rose, and, once they were out of the kitchen and down the steps, she looped her arm through Lorena's. The heat of the day was upon the town, and they tried to stay in the shadow of the buildings. Even so, they were sweating profusely by the time Mary turned her in the direction of the café.

Lorena dug in her heels, balking at walking up the back steps. "Oh, no, I can't," she protested.

"Of course you can. You're family," Mary soothed, giving her a push. "Come, Lorena. Deirdre is as welcoming as we are, as you well know."

"I work for her," Lorena said, flushing from embarrassment rather than the heat.

"No, you are her sister." Mary gave her a stern look, as though she were a recalcitrant child in need of scolding. When Lorena ascended the steps, Mary beamed at her. "Good girl." Upon entering the kitchen, Mary gave a swift shake of her head to forestall Deirdre from asking questions, smiling at Deirdre as she asked, "Would you mind if Lorena and Declan stayed in one of your guest rooms for a bit? I'll help clean it and ensure they're comfortable."

Deirdre stared in surprise at the two women for a moment, before shaking her head. "Of course not. We've plenty of room, and any O'Rourke is always welcome. I'd think you'd want the other spare room for Gavin, as I doubt Declan would want to be separated from him."

Mary nodded her thanks. "Aren't you a wise lass," she said in approval of Deirdre's thinking. She looked around the kitchen and winked at her daughter-in-law. "I'll have a few of the lads here soon to help with the dishes." At Deirdre's relieved sigh, Mary caressed her arm. "Ask us for help, love. There's no shame in needin' our support when you're busy."

Deirdre nodded. "I'll need it for the next few weeks. We're busier than we've ever been."

Mary nodded. "Grand. Maggie and I'll be here in the morning. And I'll have the lads here soon, after I ensure Lorena is settled." Mary urged Lorena up the stairs. "Now isn't this too large a space for just a husband and wife?" Mary asked, as she stared around the large living area over the café.

Lorena shook her head. "I'd never want to argue with you in front of family, Mary, but I couldn't possibly impose ..."

Mary firmed her jaw and gripped Lorena's shoulders. "'Tis no imposition. They've the rooms just gatherin' dust, until they finally bless me with grandchildren. Now come," she said, urging Lorena to follow her as she opened two doors. "These are the guest rooms. Which one do you like?"

"Either," Lorena said, with an indifferent shrug. "I know I won't be here long, so it doesn't matter."

Mary gave her a look indicating she was nearly fed up with her self-pity, but she didn't press the issue. "I'd take this one. 'Tis a bit quieter." She puttered around, wiping away imaginary flecks of dust and tucking in a bed corner. "There. 'Tis all set for you and Declan."

Lorena put her hand on Mary's arm as she bustled past. "Mary, … thank you." Her voice choked with tears; she was unable to say any more.

Mary pulled her in for a hug, patting her back. "All will be well. It might take some time, and you'll have to be honest in a way that terrifies you." She paused as she looked deeply into Lorena's eyes. "But you'll discover life with a man like my Declan is worth it, once you overcome your fears and accept what's already growin' between you."

Lorena watched her depart, struggling to find the courage she knew she needed to make things right with Declan.

"**M**um!" Declan called out, as he barreled into the kitchen at the big family home. He gasped in a breath, as he met Maggie's disapproving gaze and as his mother looked at him with concern. "Is Lo here?"

"I never thought you'd lose your wife on the first day of your marriage," his father said from the kitchen doorway. He looked at his son with a glower, as he shook his head, his eyes glowing with frank disappointment.

"I didn't lose her," Declan protested, flushing as he admitted, "I just don't know where she went."

Maggie made a noise of disgust, as she slipped from the room, their father following her.

"Mum?" Declan asked, as Mary dried her hands on a towel after washing dishes. He followed her to the large empty table, sitting beside her.

"You ran away at the first sign of trouble, didn't you, lad?" Mary asked in a soft voice laced with sadness. "Rather than face your fears, and hers, you ran."

"Mum," he murmured again, letting out a deep breath, as he rubbed at his forehead. "Aye, I ran. I ran when I realized I'd been played a fool. Again."

"A fool?" Mary shook her head. "No, Declan, you're no fool, and you never have been. You're trusting and eager to love, but that doesn't make you foolish." She gripped his hand. "Don't let the world harden you, my boy." She gazed at him. "And don't let the words of a heartless woman convince you of things that aren't true."

He gaped at her. "How did you know?"

"I haven't always been with your da," she whispered. "Francois was, … well, worse than a bully. And I believed his lies for too long. Your da has helped me see them for what they were. Lies."

"A.J. says I put too much credence in fear."

Mary winced and nodded. "What do you believe, love?" she whispered, as she ran a hand over his head and let it settle at his nape. When she met his haunted gaze, her eyes filled. "I'm sorry, Declan." She pulled him close into her embrace. "I'm sorry for ever bein' separated from you."

"I know, Mum," he whispered. "I hate that I doubted you'd be here. That I doubted you'd accept Gavin and show joy in him."

She cupped his face. "He is your son," she said in a tone that brooked no argument. "Just as Lorena is your wife. You have to face your fears and stop running, Declan."

He nodded. "Where is she, Mum?"

"At your new home. For now." She smiled when he furrowed his brow in bewilderment. "You're staying in rooms above the café. Ardan and Deirdre have space." She shook her head to quiet any protest. "There's a room for Gavin, so you won't be separated from him, although I know he'll still spend a lot of his time with us." Her sweet smile burst forth. "I can't imagine much time away from the little prince."

Declan pulled her close. "Thank you, Mum." He held her for a long moment, before departing to reunite with his wife.

~

Declan eased open the guest bedroom door in Ardan and Deirdre's house. His ears still rang from the admonishments he'd received from Deirdre in the café below, and he hoped never to see such disappointment in his father's gaze ever again. His anxiety eased at the sight of his wife huddled under the sheet, her back to the door. After a moment, his uneasiness rose when he saw her back shake with suppressed sobs.

"Lo?" he whispered, shutting the door behind him and moving to the bed. "Forgive me." The bed dipped with his weight, and he raised his hand to run over her back. When she flinched at the light touch of his fingertips, he dropped his hand by his side.

Rather than turn to face him, she remained on her side, her shoulders shaking. Declan sighed, kicking off his boots, shedding his shirt and pants, before climbing under the sheet in his underclothes. "Lo," he murmured, wrapping his arm around her waist to tug her up against him. "I'm sorry. I was jealous an' mean." He sighed, resting his forehead between her shoulder blades. "All I could see was the past, where I'd been played false. I feared I'd been tricked again."

"I am not her," she gasped out, her words emerging in stuttering pants between her sobs.

"Aye," he whispered. "Just as I'm not him." He paused a long moment before murmuring, "Josiah." As her arms flailed about, hitting him in his stomach and chest, he grunted and rolled away from her. As the waning daylight entered the large windows, he met her horrified gaze.

"How do you know that name?" she asked. "Who told you?"

Instead of replying, he traced soft fingers down her cheeks, smoothing away her tears in an attempt to soothe her. He frowned as he saw more tears pool in her beautiful eyes, before spilling down to meet his thumbs.

"Winnifred?" At the shake of his head, Lorena paled and gave out a broken-hearted moan. "Phoebe?"

"Oh, love, come here," he coaxed, urging her forward and into his strong arms. "*You* told me," he breathed, as he kissed the top of her head. "Last night, just as you tumbled into sleep. You called me his name."

As she attempted to wriggle away from him, Declan's hold on her tightened. "I couldn't have. I wouldn't have. I never speak his name." She flushed as she met her husband's pained expression.

"You did," Declan said, as he ran a hand over the side of her head. "And I realized that you'd never wanted me. You'd been dreaming of him the entire time."

"No!" Lorena gasped, as she pressed up, pushing against his strong chest. "That's not how it is." She shook her head. "Not anymore."

"Not anymore," he said in a sorrow-laced voice. His fingers continued to play with her hair, as he stared deeply into her eyes. "Why did you marry me, Lorena? You already vowed you'd never love me. I thought I could accept passion and a woman dedicated to my son. But I fear I accepted a fool's bargain."

Lorena flinched and rested her head on his chest, accepting she couldn't escape his gentle hold. And accepting the need to talk, at least a little, about her past. "I loved before. And I know love only brings pain and suffering. I have no desire to live through that again."

Declan rested in quiet contemplation for many moments, the only sounds in the room their breathing. He traced patterns over her back and ran his fingers through her hair. Finally he murmured, "Does my da's love provoke pain and sufferin' in my mum?" He shook his head. "Not bein' together caused them their misery."

"I'm not an O'Rourke," she protested.

"Ah, love, that's where you're wrong. You very much are an O'Rourke. Not simply because you married me. You've been one since they took you in and since you accepted Da's advice and Mum's love."

"You don't understand," she whispered. "I've done despicable things. I'm a horrible person. You can't care for me. I won't let you."

He placed fingers over her lips, silencing her. "*Shh*, love. I hate that you think such things about yourself, but I won't listen to you speak about yourself in such a way. You're good and kind and have so much to give." He paused as he gazed into her eyes. "But *you* have to believe that. I can't force you." He kissed her forehead, before resting his against hers. "We both have tales to tell, love. I'll wait until you're ready to tell me yours."

She hiccupped, easing away from his gentle hold, whispering, "Did you seek me out tonight because your family shamed you into finding me?"

His eyes blazed as he shook his head. "You're my wife. I belong by your side, as you belong by mine. I hope to never spend a night apart from you." He waited until he saw her softly smile at his words. "Come, love. Let me hold you while you sleep, as I should have done last night." He sighed with contentment when she rested her head against his chest, her breathing slowing into a soft cadence that lulled him into sleep.

I n the O'Rourke kitchen at the big table, Lorena sat beside Declan the following morning, leaning against his side. She wished she could say she was secure in his affection. Secure in his love. However, she was secure in his loyalty to her and his promise that he would give her the time she needed to tell him the truths written on her heart. That patience endeared him in a way nothing else could.

As she stole glances at the happy couples scattered around the table, Lorena realized with a shock that envy no longer ate at her. Instead a nascent hope filled her that she could one day be as they were. Committed to another's happiness as readily as she guarded her own. She watched as Phoebe flirted with Eamon and as Seamus teased Mary, a deep joy welling inside Lorena to be a part of such a family.

Biting her lip, Lorena battled a smile, as she watched Maggie and Dunmore continue their unique courtship.

"I wonder how long until they give in to the inevitable," Declan whispered in her ear.

She smiled up at him, shrugging. "Something or someone might have to give them a push. They seem to enjoy their dance."

"Ah, but what they haven't figured out, or he hasn't been smart enough to convince wee Maggie of yet, is that the dance doesn't end when you marry a fine woman." Declan's blue eyes shone with sincerity as he stared at her.

"Declan," she breathed, her hand clasping his under the table.

Eamon cleared his throat, as Phoebe blushed. "Ah, I have an announcement to make, an' we cannot wait any longer to share the news with you." He grinned when Maggie squealed with excitement as she squirmed in her seat, her eyes glowing with anticipation. Eamon nodded. "Yes, Phoebe and I are expecting our first child."

Lorena watched as Maggie gave a yelp of joy and as Mary rushed to the table to embrace each of them. Soon everyone had encircled the couple, talking, laughing, and exulting at the news. The outpouring of love and support was as expected from the O'Rourkes, as they didn't know any other way to show their love. However, Lorena watched in wonder at the outpouring of affection for Phoebe.

Finally they settled in for breakfast again. Lorena fought a giggle as she watched Maggie cast covetous eyes in Dunmore's direction. Lorena's giggle turned to a stifled moan when Winnifred entered the kitchen, a satisfied gleam in her gaze.

As Winnifred's grating voice called out, "Oh, look at all the happy couples," interrupting the peaceful chatter, Lorena froze. "Oh no."

"Everything will be fine," Declan soothed.

"You don't understand," Lorena said in a pleading voice. "Believe in me, not her." She spun to face her sister, as Winnifred continued to talk.

"I can't believe another O'Rourke has been taken in by a Mortimer sister. But then I suppose gullibility is the most predominant O'Rourke trait." Winnifred smiled with insincere friendliness to everyone seated around the table, ignoring Seamus's threatening glower and the blatant disgust in Mary's gaze. "Although I am surprised that one who claims to adore his son with such a desperate fervency would deign to align himself with a woman who abandoned her child without a second thought."

"Winnie," Lorena begged, her eyes rounded, her breath leaving her in a *whoosh* as though she had just been punched. "No, please no."

Taking no notice of her sister's panic, Winnifred continued in a singsong voice. "I'd hate to think what could happen to that poor boy. Lo's never been known for her constancy."

Lorena stared dazedly at the family seated around the table, seeing condemnation, confusion, and contempt. She looked to Phoebe, blanching when her sister stared at her as though she were a stranger. Finally she looked at Declan, any color leeching away as he stared at her with no warmth or understanding. "I … I'm sorry," she gasped, wrenching her hand from Declan's and racing away.

She barreled down the steps and headed to the café. As she neared the rear door, she paused, gasping for breath. She prayed she'd hear footsteps racing after her, Declan's voice calling out to her. Instead all she heard were the common sounds from the town. Nothing more.

She paused in her flight away from the O'Rourke house, as she realized she was returning to another O'Rourke home. Her chest heaved from the emotional blow rendered by her sister and the emotional devastation due to Declan letting her go. She glanced around, hating that she felt aimless and homeless at the same time, when recently she had felt full of purpose and hope. Rather than return to the room she had shared with Declan, in his brother's home, she spun away, determined to find another place of refuge.

CHAPTER 12

"Declan, sit," Seamus commanded. "And you," he snapped, as he pointed his finger at Winnifred, "cease your mindless prattle about matters that don't concern you. You might believe you understand what your sister suffered, but I can assure you that we never understand another's misery."

"Suffering?" Winnifred scoffed with a roll of her eyes. "Good riddance, I say. Who'd want to be saddled with a brat?"

Mary gasped, lurching to her feet, and, before anyone understood her intent, she slapped Winnifred across the cheek. "I've had enough of you," she said in a low voice, all the more potent for its restrained tone. "I've had enough of you sowing your discontent, your doubt, and your spite among those I love. You are no O'Rourke, and you are not welcome among us."

"What?" Winnifred gasped. "How can you punish me for exposing the truth? I was protecting your son."

Seamus slammed his hand down on the table and rose. The room went deathly quiet, as everyone waited to see what he would do. "Nay, lass, you were spouting *your* truth. *Your* venom." He stood beside Mary, wrapping an arm around her shoulder. "And I'll always support my Mary's decisions. You've never treated your sisters, or my Mary and my Maggie, with anything but contempt. You have no place with us."

"Aren't you always proclaiming you won't be alone? That you'll always have someone to look out for you?" Declan motioned to the door. "Now's your time to prove that belief true."

Winnifred gaped at the family, her gaze finally falling on Finn, who sat with a clenched jaw and flashing blue eyes filled with pain and disappointment. With a show of bravado, Winnifred tilted her chin up and smiled. "I've never needed any of you. Only a fool turns her back on free lodging and meals." She stomped away to her room, Maggie on her heels.

"Miss Maggie?" Dunmore asked, as she was about to slip from the room.

Maggie smiled at him and then her family in general. "I'm fine. I want to ensure she doesn't try to take anything that's not hers." She winked at them, before heading upstairs.

Seamus let out a deep breath and focused on his son. "Declan, you must find your bride. And reassure her that Winnifred will not be here to harm her again."

Mary stepped forward to grip his arm. "We chose Lorena."

Declan nodded. "Aye," he whispered, thankful when he heard the soft chatter resume, as his siblings and sisters-in-law began to eat breakfast again. "The last thing she said to me was to have faith in her. I fear she believes I didn't because I didn't leap to her defense. And I didn't chase after her."

Seamus scratched at his head. "Aye, she might. But we had to clean house, and you needed to be present. Winnifred has to understand you would defend your wife."

"You were in agreement with us," Mary said.

Declan nodded. "Thanks, Mum. Da." He spun on his heel, slipping from the room.

Seamus sighed, wrapping his arms around Mary, as she rested her head against his shoulder. "I fear I made a mistake preventing Declan from racing after her. Her fears will only become more entrenched."

Mary made a soothing noise, as she kissed his cheek. "Then 'twill only be all the sweeter when she lets them go."

Seamus kissed her forehead. "Aye," he murmured, as he watched Dunmore leave, and he lost his opportunity to speak with the stagecoach driver about the risk facing Maggie. He made a silent promise he would have a family meeting the next time Dunmore was in town.

~

Lorena stood near the levee, watching men load steamboats for the return trip to Saint Louis. She fought a yearning to have the money to purchase a return ticket. To sail away and to leave this heartache behind. She rubbed at her chest, acknowledging that she would carry this pain with her, no matter how far away she ran.

"I see you've come to realize your mistake," her uncle called out, as he approached. Today he wore a tan suit with a peacock-blue waistcoat.

She closed her eyes a moment at the sound of his voice, only opening them when she sensed him standing in front of her. "I've made no mistake. I merely desired fresh air."

"When O'Rourkes want peace and quiet, they go to that stream." He pointed in the direction away from town. He shook his head, as he stared at her with cunning intensity. "No, you want to escape." He leaned forward with an avaricious smile. "Don't you realize I can still offer you just what you want?"

Lorena took a step away from him, her shoulders back, as she faced him and attempted to mimic Maggie's bravery. "I already have what I want."

He snorted out a laugh, rolling his eyes, as he hitched his hands into the suspenders keeping his pants up. "If you had what you wanted, you'd be in your husband's bed right now, and he wouldn't be disgusted by you."

Lorena paled, as her eyes rounded in shock. "How ...?"

"At least one member of your family understands the meaning of loyalty." He took a step toward her. "Cease your foolishness, and join me. You'll have your money soon enough to do what you want."

Shaking her head, over and over again, Lorena stuttered out, "No, no, no." She wrapped her arms around her waist. "I'll never join you. I'll never be what you want me to be."

He growled as he reached for her. "Don't you see you already are? Undesired by your husband? Abandoned days after the wedding?" He shook his head, his eyes gleaming with pity. "You're pathetic." He looked around, smiling with feigned amity and innocence. "Where are the vaunted O'Rourkes now? They don't seem so eager to protect you."

"I won't go with you. I won't do what you want," she whispered.

"Missus!" a familiar voice called out, a moment before he gripped her arm and kept her from taking an involuntary step toward her uncle. "Sure is nice to see such a beautiful woman out on such a fine mornin'." A.J. stared from Lorena to her uncle with a guileless gaze.

"Leave us," Uriah snapped. "This is a family matter, and you have no business interrupting us."

"Family?" A.J. asked with a quirk of his brow, his hold on Lorena tightening and his muscles quivering, as though expecting a fight. "Well, if you was family, you'd have been at the weddin'. Seein' as you wasn't there, I'm more family than you. Good day to you, *Urea*."

A giggle burst forth from Lorena at A.J.'s name for her uncle, and he winked at her as he led her away from the levee and her uncle and farther down the riverfront. "He ain't so scary when ye realize he's nothing more than a man filled with too much of a bad thing." He winked at her. "Now come tell Uncle A.J. what's taken away your bloom."

She rested her head against his shoulder, sighing as she looked out at the river. The constancy of the river should bring her solace. Instead it made her feel a restlessness. As though she wished she could be in motion too. "I made a mistake. Mistakes. And I'll never stop paying for them."

"Ah, missus, we all make mistakes. Sometimes we learn from them. Sometimes we regret them until the day we die. But we have to overcome them, so they don't overcome us." He had shifted so he could stare into her eyes, his countenance uncharacteristically serious. "Nothin' that we've done is unpardonable."

Shaking her head, she said, "You can say that because you don't know what I've done."

He heaved out a deep breath, clamping his jaw together, as though his mouth gripped a pipe. After a long moment, he murmured, "I'd bet it had somethin' to do with a child."

Her cheeks lost whatever color she had regained after leaving her uncle's company, while gaping at A.J. in dawning horror. "How? Why?" She wrenched her arm free of his and took a stumbling step backward. "Is that all you men do? Gossip?"

A.J. shook his head and sighed. "No, missus. We don't. We chatter on about unimportant topics. You womenfolk talk about the essential things."

She stared at him quizzically. "Unimportant?"

He waved his hand around and stared at her in all seriousness. "Listen to me well, missus. I know what it is to suffer the pain of a baby lost before they were little more than a dream. The pain of wishin' for somethin' that's never comin'." He nodded as he met her sorrow-filled gaze. "My Bessie an' me can't have little 'uns. It's the sorry truth."

He paused a long moment, waiting for her to speak. When she remained silent, he took in a breath, his brown eyes gleaming with his fervency. "Standin' here, right now, you have a choice. You can either cling to your pain or let it go. You can't have the sorrow of your past as yer bedfellow each night, while tryin' to woo a husband. Makes for a crowded bed."

Unheeded, a tear trickled down her cheek. "I'm so sorry, Mr. A.J." She attempted a smile, as he looked at her in a perplexed manner. "So sorry for what you suffered." She held a hand to her chest. "There is no worse pain."

A.J. sighed, nodding a few times, before shaking his head. "Ah, ye're right an' wrong, missus. The pain is fierce an' near eats you up inside. But it was worse seein' how my Bessie suffered." He shook his head. "No worse anguish than that. And there ain't nothin' I wouldn't do to make her smile."

Lorena's breath stuttered, as she whispered, "The difference is, you had no choice over what happened to your baby."

He gazed deeply into her eyes. "Havin' spent time with your sisters, I'd bet all the money I'll make as a captain this year that you had as little choice about losin' your babe as my Bessie did. Too often circumstances are out of our control."

Lorena gazed at him mournfully. "I've never forgiven myself."

Nodding, A.J. sighed. "Well, you have to, missus. Lookin' to your husband for *absalvation* won't bring you peace."

"*Absalvation?*" Lorena whispered, her brows furrowed, as she focused on a problem other than her past or her present troubles with Declan. "*Absolution* or *salvation?*"

He beamed at her. "I knew the smartest lady in town could figure out my words." He winked at her and winged out his arm. "Come. Let me escort you back to the café. You've let your husband fret long enough." He shook his head when she began to protest. "And he's frettin', missus, so don't argue with me."

Lorena walked beside the man who acted like a benevolent uncle, feeling lighter in spirit than she had in years. Although she remained filled with trepidation at the thought of facing Declan, she knew he had earned the right to hear the truth from her.

Deirdre's kitchen was a beehive of activity as Declan poked his head in. She moved with effortless grace from the stove to the table to mix batter for a cake to the oven, where she checked on cooking rolls. He sniffed appreciatively, as nothing ever smelled as good as Deirdre's kitchen. Not even his mum's kitchen, although he would never admit that.

He nodded to two of his youngest brothers, who had been charged with washing dishes, forcing a smile as he saw Bryan and Henri whispering to each other as they scrubbed pans and rinsed them dry. "Lads," he said, his smile broadening as they flushed at his appearance.

"She's not here!" Bryan called out. He had a youthful vivacity about him and retained an optimistic joyful outlook about each day, as though looking forward to every adventure to come his way. Declan found himself envious of Bryan's naiveté and secretly hoped his brother never experienced heartache. He dreaded the day Bryan ever had a cynical glint in his green eyes.

"Thanks, Bryan," he said. "I suppose you're in the middle of the breakfast rush," he said to Deirdre, ignoring his two brothers, who began whispering to each other again. He attempted to match her smile but understood he failed when he saw concern bloom in her beautiful gaze.

Although his eldest brother Ardan had been married to Deirdre for nearly two years, Declan barely knew her, as he'd been away the entire time. He studied her a moment. A beautiful woman with red-gold hair, dusted with flour, and cognac-colored eyes that Declan feared saw too much and gave little away, Declan realized she was the perfect woman for his brother. Her competence and quiet confidence were a match for his serious eldest brother.

He hoped the small lines at the corner of her mouth and eyes were due to the laughter she shared with Ardan. For Ardan needed laughter and joy in his life.

"Deirdre," he murmured, with a deferential nod.

"She'll come back, Declan," she said in her husky voice. She nodded to the younger brothers, answering his unspoken question about how she knew of the calamitous breakfast. "Never doubt she cares."

"I don't know what to do," he said, as he sat with a sigh. He half smiled as she set a full plate of food in front of him.

"Food makes everything better." She smiled at him, although her concern for him lingered in her gaze. "She's suffered, Declan. I don't know what, but it's a deep hurt. Give her time, patience, and under-standing." When he remained silent, she said in a low voice, "Those are gifts I have found O'Rourke men give the women they love. And they are priceless."

His head jerked up at the word *love*, but he didn't contradict her assertion. She squeezed his shoulder, before continuing her work in the kitchen. After wolfing down the delicious breakfast, he strummed his fingers on the table, as he waited for Ardan. Although he wished Ardan would stop chattering away with the customers, Declan knew that was an important part of his role, and he knew Ardan enjoyed it.

Declan battled his mounting impatience for the busy morning rush at the café to finish, so that Ardan could help him search for Lorena. He turned to the back door when it opened, then bolted to his feet, racing to it. "Lo!" He reached out to pull her into his embrace, his arms hanging in the air beside her, as he froze at the last second, uncertain she wanted him to touch her.

"Declan," she whispered, taking the final step so she rested against him. At her soft sigh of relief when his arms clasped her gently to him, he let out a groan of relief.

"Don't do that to me again, Lo," he pleaded in her ear, his breath tickling her sensitive skin and blowing on the fine hair of her nape. "Don't scare me like that again."

She pressed back, gazing deeply into his eyes. "Scare you?" At the terror in his gaze, she cupped his cheek and shook her head. "I've had a lovely chat with Mr. A.J."

Declan glanced beside her toward the older man, who he was beginning to regard as another benevolent older sibling. "I'm glad."

"Ah, yes, the missus an' I had a fine chat by the Missouri. Once we separated ourselves from her uncle, that is." A.J.'s eyes gleamed with warning, as he met Declan's furious gaze.

Now focusing on his wife, he cupped her faced and asked, "Your uncle dared to speak with you?" At her resigned nod, he forced a calm expression. "Come. Sit. Deirdre, would you mind feeding Lorena as well?" With a smile to her, he turned to Lorena. "I know you didn't have much to eat at the house."

She sat on one of the stools around the large kitchen island, watching as Deirdre scooped out a generous serving of eggs, potatoes, and bacon, with a biscuit on the side. "Thank you," she murmured in an abashed tone, as she kept her head ducked, a wave of shyness enveloping her. When A.J. regaled Deirdre and the younger boys with a tale about a three-legged cat, Lorena whispered to Declan, "I'm sorry."

Her husband brushed at the hair on her cheeks and shook his head. "Sorry? Why are you sorry, love?"

She tapped her fork on the plate, before taking a deep breath to face his concerned gaze. "For not being honest from the beginning. I should have been. You would never have married me—"

"*Shh,*" he admonished, placing a finger over her lips. "You know no such thing. And this discussion is best had in private." He nodded to her full plate. "Come. Eat your fill." He rested his palm on her knee and gave it a gentle squeeze, as he joined in chatting with A.J. about life in Fort Benton.

Lorena took an obliging bite of food, closing her eyes with a groan of pleasure as she realized just how hungry she was and how delicious Deirdre's food was. She gobbled down the entire plate of food, as she listened to Declan and Mr. A.J. speak nonsense, her anxiety about what was to come easing with each passing moment.

D eclan stared out the window in the bedroom he shared with Lorena in the rooms above the kitchen and café. He'd had a few moments with Gavin, before Samantha had taken him to his parents' house, and seeing his son had soothed a little of the ache in his soul.

Although he had always believed himself a patient man, today he found that attribute to be in short supply. With a sudden ferocity, he wanted to know everything he could about his wife. Her childhood. Her friends. Her first love. With a sigh, he rubbed at his head, as he'd seen his father do too many times to count. Most important of all, he wanted Lorena to trust him enough to tell him about her baby.

With an impatience borne of anxiety about his own hidden truths, he paced away from the window to the bed and then back again. With a sigh, he leaned against the window frame, his gaze distant and his mind filled with all he wished he could forget. All he knew he had to tell his wife to show his faith in her.

"I'm sorry," she said in a low contrite voice that shook from behind him.

He spun to face her and stared at her, as though she were an apparition for a moment. Then he smiled. "Don't be. I've been anxious to see you." He approached her slowly, afraid to startle her. "To hold you." Some of his tension eased when she smiled, opening her arms to him.

With a grateful groan, he wrapped her in his strong embrace. "Whatever you have to tell me, I will honor it. And you. I will not judge you for what happened in the past." He looked deeply into her green eyes. "As I hope you will not judge me."

She shook her head, her arms around his waist squeezing him tight.

"Will you listen?" he whispered.

"Of course," she said, as she kissed his chest. "Whatever you have to say will not change how I feel about you, Declan. I already know you to be a remarkable man."

He closed his eyes and shook his head. "I fear you will think differently when I am done with my tale." He eased them onto the bed to sit side by side but then rose to pace in front of her, the words bursting forth in a torrent, as though a dam had ruptured.

"I met a woman in Saint Louis early last spring. About a year and a half ago. Magnolia Harding. I thought she was the most beautiful creature I'd ever laid eyes on. Gold ringlets and blue eyes the color of a robin's egg. A dazzling deceitful beauty. I was blinded by her meaningless charm. Her meaningless flirtations. I never saw below the surface."

He fisted his hands and hit his thigh as he walked, his pacing continuing, until he spun to face Lorena, his eyes blazing with fury and loathing. It was impossible to determine if the loathing was for himself or Magnolia. "I wasn't cunning enough to see through her charade. To see she was only interested in whatever riches I might have. That she wished I had my own business and was disdainful I worked with my family. I ignored her prattle about the number of servants I had or how much I had saved in a bank."

When he paused, she whispered, "Why, Declan? She doesn't seem at all the type of woman you would like." She flushed as he stared at her for a long moment. "Forgive me for presuming ..."

"No," he said, as he held out a hand in her direction. "You should presume. You're my wife. You're the type of woman I should have always sought." He frowned as he saw her flush and duck her head, as though ashamed of his regard for her. "I was blinded by her beauty and her flirtatious manner and didn't have the sense to notice her beauty was a thin varnish covering a black soul. I was stunned that a woman every man desired would want a man like me."

"A man like you?" she asked, her head jerking up to meet his tormented gaze. "I don't understand. Why would you ever doubt who you are?"

Declan approached the bed and sat beside her, gently clasping her hand. "You've heard the tales. Of how my own brother married the first woman meant for me. And then Ardan found love. I thought, surely, as the third brother, I should be the next to marry. To find a woman to match the women my brothers had wed and marry her. I was desperate to prove myself."

"Prove yourself?" she whispered. "I don't understand."

He took a deep breath and gazed deeply into her eyes before he whispered, "Prove that I was worthy of loving."

"Worthy of loving?" she repeated. When he jerked away, as though she had slapped him, she launched herself at him, wrapping her arms and legs around him, until she sat on his lap and held him close. "No, you misunderstand. You're such a worthy man. One of the worthiest men I've ever met. If she were so feebleminded that she couldn't understand that ..." She shrugged.

Declan rested his head on her shoulder. "I cut my hair. Shaved off my beard. Traded in my backwoodsman clothes for suits. Everything I could think of to please her."

143

She ran her fingers through his short hair. "Oh, you silly man, don't you know that none of that matters? What matters is who you are here." She held a hand over his heart. "If she couldn't see that, she didn't deserve you."

His eyes glistened as he stared at her. "*I* couldn't see it, Lorena," he said in a low tone. "In the end, 'tis all that matters." He closed his eyes. "I was a fool for her. Fought my brothers over her. Refused to listen to reason. Was determined to prove I could be loved." He cleared his throat. "Forced them to leave me behind, while I chased after her."

"Why?" Lorena whispered. "Your family is so close. Why would you push them away?"

"Aye, our family is close. We love each other something fierce, and accept almost everyone." His expression clouded as he thought about Colleen, Connor and Jacques. "When I left for Saint Louis, two of my brothers had found women to love, women as worthy as my mum. They experienced hardships, aye, but they still made love seem effortless. I'd heard stories about how Da saw mum across a room and knew he'd marry her. I thought I'd have the same story to tell after meeting Magnolia. I was a fool."

"No, Declan, you weren't a fool. You were hopeful. And lonely."

He shrugged, his motion jostling her on his lap. "If I listened to my brothers, then I had to acknowledge what they said was true. That Magnolia used me. That I was nothing to her. And I couldn't bear it."

She made a sound of protest, as she pressed herself closer to him. "What happened?" she whispered. "You're here, with your son, without her."

"I tracked her to New Orleans, with the man she truly loved. Andre Martin." His hold on her tightened. "She was shocked to see me. Astonished I had followed her." His jaw clenched and unclenched. "They were trying to dupe another man. A richer man. And I was in the way." He shook his head with impatience. "No, that's not true. Her being pregnant with Gavin was in the way. They had no use for a baby who would prevent her from finding another benefactor, while she continued with her lover on the side."

He stared at her with a nearly unbearable sadness. "I'd discerned by then Gavin wasn't mine. There's no way he could have been. I met her in early March, and he was born in early August."

"What would she do?"

"If she could, sell him as soon as she gave birth. If not, leave him on a street corner," Declan said in a low, irate voice. "Hope someone would find him and care for him. Or take him to an orphanage." He stared at her, his gaze filled with self-hatred. "How could I have ever esteemed a woman who was so heartless? She died in childbirth, and I feel such relief knowing she's dead. And such guilt at that relief. I shouldn't rejoice at another's demise."

Cupping his face, she leaned forward, until their foreheads touched. "Forgive yourself, Declan, for caring for her. You didn't know any better. You wanted love. To be loved." She gazed at him with a mixture of marvel and disbelief. "I can't believe the man you are today after having suffered so."

"Aye, well, I fear I've not changed as much as I'd hoped."

She stilled, staring into his eyes. "What is it you fear?" she asked, as she traced a hand over his chest. "About me?"

A long silence ensued before he admitted, "That you want Gavin more than you'll ever want me." He held his breath, as she gaped at him. "I see how you watch him. As though he were every dream you ever wanted wrapped up in a perfect little bundle." He closed his eyes. "I know we're married, but I need to know you didn't marry me simply for Gavin. Or my family."

She sat upright, pushing away from him. "You have a very low opinion of me, don't you?" She swiped away a tear. "First I covet your son. Then your family. With no regard for you?"

He grabbed her and rolled with her until she rested caged underneath him, his weight held off her by his knees and elbows. "Dammit, want me at least as much as you want them. Please." His blue eyes sparkled with desperation and the tears he fought to prevent from falling.

"Of course I want you," she said. "How could I not want you, you remarkable man?" Her hand rose to caress his cheek. "I will always have trouble believing you want me."

He leaned forward, his nose brushing over hers. His gaze softened, as he saw her eyes flutter closed, and a contented smile bloomed. With a subtle shift, he brushed his lips over hers reverently. "I will always want you, Lo." He leaned away. "I hope, in time, you'll trust me with what you believe brings you shame." He gazed deeply into her beautiful eyes. "And learn that nothing you have done will ever make me think less of you."

He frowned as her eyes welled with tears, and he rolled so she rested her head on his strong chest. "There's a love," he murmured, kissing her head, while running his fingers over her back. "There's a love." He held her as sobs burst forth, wrenched from her.

She clung to him, her back heaving and her breath hitching, as she soaked his shirt. "Forgive me," she gasped out. "I'm so embarrassed."

"No, love," he whispered. "This is what marriage is all about. Sharing ourselves. Our joy. Our grief. Our hopes. Our pain." He tilted his head, so he could see her eyes. "At least I hope 'tis how it is."

She raised a quivering hand to caress his cheek. "I never dared dream I could have this. Not since …" She broke off and buried her face in his chest.

"*Shh*, love, we have time. There's no rush," he murmured, as he held her until she tumbled into a restful sleep.

CHAPTER 13

The following day, Lorena sat in the O'Rourke kitchen, sipping a cup of tea. She knew she needed to head to the burned-out shell of her bookstore and begin the cleanup, but she didn't have the heart to see the charred remains of her dreams. Although she knew she should do something, be an active member of the family and help in some way, she remained seated at the table, her mind distant.

All she could think about was Declan. Her mind was filled with the story he had told about his treacherous relationship with Magnolia Harding. Lorena gave silent thanks that he had left Saint Louis to return home, that they had become reluctant friends, and that they had married. With a shiver, she imagined what his reaction would be when she told him about her past. For the first time, she felt the stirrings of an inner strength to even dare speaking of all that haunted her.

"Are you shiverin', love?" Mary asked, as she entered the kitchen. She rested the back of her hand against Lorena's forehead. "You've no fever. Are you ailin'?" Mary peered at her with unconcealed concern.

"No, not ailing," Lorena said, her fingers playing with the teacup. "I'm trying to marshal courage, and I'm finding it difficult."

Mary stared at her with understanding. "I've found the imagining is almost always worse than reality. Almost." A shadow crossed her expression. "As I'm sure you've heard, I had a difficult second marriage. That reality was worse than imaginings." She shuddered. "What I've found since returnin' to my life with Seamus and our children is that I can't allow my fears of what *might* occur to ruin the happiness that I am *actually* experiencing."

Lorena furrowed her brows and shook her head.

After settling across from Lorena, Mary linked her fingers together around her mug, gazing at the woman she considered her newest daughter. "I've discovered in the past two years that I must believe I deserve the joy and the delight I feel every day. That I shouldn't cling to a shred of doubt, fearing that something or someone will come to rip away from me everything I hold most precious. I've learned the true meaning of faith."

Her eyes filling with tears, Lorena sniffled. "I fear I lost any faith years ago, and I won't ever be able to recover it."

"Ah, lass, you will," Mary soothed. She paused, granting them a few moments of quiet contemplation. "However, not only must you trust in Declan, you must trust in yourself. And believe you are worthy of all you desire."

"How?" Lorena whispered. "How do you recover that faith? That belief?"

Mary reached forward, clasping one of Lorena's hands. "You must forgive yourself for whatever you believe is unforgiveable. You must let go of the self-hatred." She paused. "I know how hard it can be." Her hazel eyes glowed with regret and sorrow. "Although you see harmony between Seamus and me, 'twasn't always the case. I was riddled with fear and insecurity. I had chosen the best I could, after discovering my babe and me alone in Montreal, but I carried a terrible burden of doubt that I hadn't tried harder to find a better man. A more worthy man to care for my wee babe and me. Instead I found myself with a brute of a man."

Lorena whispered, "How did you forgive yourself?"

"I won't lie, Lorena. It took time—and the constancy of Seamus's love and support. But I overcame my fears and my feeling of unworthiness." Her eyes glowed as she began to speak of Seamus. "He kissed my scars," she whispered. "Touched me with reverence, when I'd only known pain for so many years." She sniffled. "'Twas a balm for my weary soul."

"Oh, Mary," Lorena murmured. "He's a wonderful man."

"Aye, he is. As is my Declan. Trust him. Believe in his regard for you. Let go of the past, so you can build a future with my son."

Lorena sat on the bed in the room she shared with Declan in Ardan and Deirdre's home. Filtered sunlight from lace curtains speckled the room, with the curtains billowing every few moments from the soft wind. In her hands, she held a folded slip of paper. Rather than open it to read the missive for the thousandth time, she closed her eyes and imagined long-ago scenes. Her first dance with the man she knew she'd love until the day she died. Her first kiss. The heart-wrenching goodbye that changed her life forever.

A tear trickled down her cheek, as she felt a calm purposefulness settle over her. A serene acceptance that what she suffered did not preclude her from finding happiness again. Lorena took a deep breath and opened her eyes, gasping in surprise to find Declan calmly watching her. "Declan!"

"Yes, love," he murmured, pushing away from the doorjamb and into the room. "I'm sorry to have interrupted your interlude."

She shook her head, her hand reaching out for him. Her hand stroked down his arm, until her fingers clasped his. "No, you misunderstand," she said in a low, halting voice. With another deep breath, she looked up and met his gaze, hers filled with uncertainty and a deep vulnerability. "I was about to leave to look for you." The hope in his gaze bolstered her faltering courage. "I wanted to show you something." She held out the letter. "And then talk."

He nodded, pulling over a chair from the corner of the room, so he could sit facing her. His hands played with hers, and he showed no urgency in reading the folded piece of paper. "Only if you're certain."

She smiled at him, as a tear trickled down her cheek. "I am. It's time. I've allowed the past to shadow the future for too long. And I want, ... I want more," she said, her voice faltering, as she looked down, breaking eye contact with him.

He pressed two of his fingers under her jaw and gently canted her head up again, gazing with a deep earnestness into her eyes. "I will honor whatever you tell me. Honor you. Honor us."

She nodded. "I know. I know I can trust you. Secrets and silence have been my stalwart companions for too long." She flushed but held his gaze. "I want more."

Cupping her cheek, his fingers sliding over her soft skin in a tender caress, he leaned forward to kiss her. "I do too, love." He rubbed his nose against hers and backed away. "May I read it?"

She handed him the letter again, biting her lip and hunching her shoulders, as he took it from her.

"None of that, Lo," Declan said, as he watched her. He ran his free hand over her shoulder and rose. "Snuggle up. Let me hold you, as I read this." He kicked off his boots, scooted back in the bed, and held his arms out for her to crawl into them. When she had rested her head against his chest, he wrapped his arms around her. "Heaven," he murmured, before lifting the letter to read.

My Darling Lorena,

By the time you read this letter, I will most likely be dead. Forgive me for not being a better soldier. For not evading injury. For not coming home to you. For not fulfilling my promise of holding you in my arms until we were old and gray.

Remember me as I was—the laughing, joy-filled man who knew he had heaven within reach because he had you. Remember the times when no words were needed.

If there was one good thing I did in my life, it was loving you.

Josiah

Lorena rested, listening to the soft cadence of his heart, taking solace from him. The letter wasn't long, but a silence ensued for minutes. However, she did not feel Declan becoming tense or anxious, and she remained calm in his arms.

"Ah, love," Declan whispered. "I'm so glad for you."

"What?" she gasped, arching up and gaping at him. "How can you say that, after reading the letter?"

He smiled at her with a deep tenderness. "I feared you'd known betrayal and disillusionment, like I had. Instead you knew love. You knew what it was to be cherished."

Tears coursed down her cheeks in an uncontrollable stream. "That makes it all worse!" she cried. "To have had everything and then to lose it," she sobbed, as she fell forward.

"Ah, love, no," he crooned, as he set aside the letter and wrapped his arms around her. "No, it means you've merely forgotten the tremendous capacity for loving and for being loved that you have. You've learned to fear it, when you should celebrate it."

"It only brings pain," she stammered out.

"Not always," he whispered, as he kissed her head, his fingers playing over her back. "Not always." He held her during the many minutes she cried, understanding the need to purge her pent-up anguish.

"I loved before you," she whispered. "A man named Josiah." Her voice sputtered to a halt. "I never say his name. I've thought for so long that to say his name would be to invoke more pain."

He shifted so they lay on their sides, staring deeply into each other's eyes. "Is that it? Or is there something more?"

She flinched and then relaxed. "You won't let me hide. Not even from myself. And that's terrifying." She sniffled as another tear trickled down her cheek, whispering her thanks as he handed her a clean handkerchief. After scrubbing at her nose and cheeks, she said, "I didn't deserve his love."

Declan nodded. "Thus you had no right to say his name." His long fingers played in her loose hair, as he caressed her shoulder and arm. He gazed deeply into her eyes for a long moment. "When did you come to realize you deserved his love? That whatever befell you was a tragedy and out of your control?"

She shook her head, staring at him in wonder. "How do you know that?"

His lips quirked in a soft smile. "I know you and the woman you are. You would never intentionally harm another, even though you are desperate for approval from those you esteem. I imagine that caused you tremendous conflict, aye?"

"Aye," she whispered, as she pressed forward, resting in his arms again. "Will you listen?"

"Always."

"I met Josiah at a soiree in Saint Louis. He was like all the other handsome men in the room that day. Well dressed, smooth talking, a good dancer." She propped up on her elbows to look into Declan's gaze. "Except he didn't fawn over Mama, and he only had eyes for me. Even then, Winnifred was gorgeous, and I was surprised at his notice."

She paused, her gaze turning inward, as though envisioning distant scenes. "I remember receiving flowers from him the next day and accepting his invitation for walks in the park. Mama never thought he was good enough. He wasn't rich enough for her. But he was a successful architect and had such a vision of how things could be." The joy faded from her gaze, replaced by fear and sadness. "And then the War started."

She shrugged. "I should have felt pride that he wanted to fight for the Union. I should have knitted him socks and hidden letters in his bag, so he could find them when he was away from me." She closed her eyes. "Instead I wallowed in my misery of losing him. In my prayers the Rebs would be inept, the conflict short-lived."

She sniffled and met Declan's steadfast compassionate gaze. "The night before he was to leave, I snuck out to see him. I had to see him one more time." She sniffled and ducked her head, blushing beet red.

"And you made love," her husband murmured.

"Yes." She met his gaze with a defiant tilt of her chin. "I should feel shame. I should accept that I disgraced my family and anything that happened was my fault."

"You spout a lot of nonsense about *should*, love," Declan said in a soft voice. "You loved the man. Thought you would marry him. And he was going off to war. I'll never blame you for taking comfort nor for offering it. Only a heartless person would."

Lorena let out a mirthless laugh. "Oh, that sums up Mama. *Heart-less*. And spouting her beliefs about shame and disgrace." She fell forward, as a few more tears coursed out.

Declan wrapped his arms around her. "What more happened, love?"

"I received that letter. Only a few months after he had left, when the fighting had barely begun. I bartered everything I had to discover what hospital he was in and to travel to him." Her jaw firmed with anger. "At first they wouldn't let me see him. Said such a place was no place for a genteel woman. I was on the verge of stealing men's clothing and dressing up as a soldier, when I met the doctor's wife. She insisted I was her new assistant and helped me gain admittance."

She shuddered. "I've seen hell," she breathed. "It's a hospital where men wait to die from their wounds, as their flesh rots, and doctors have nothing to alleviate their suffering."

Swallowing, Lorena said, "I found Josiah, feverish and near death. He recognized me." She shrugged. "At least I tell myself he did." Tears tracked down her cheek. "He died an hour after I arrived."

"Oh, love," Declan murmured, wrapping her close.

"I never ... never got to tell him that we were to have a baby," she gasped. "That he was to be a papa. And I a mama." She looked at Declan. "The only solace I had was that, at least I still had a small piece of him."

Declan nodded, a tear leaking from one of his eyes, as he stroked his fingers over her cheek.

"I wrote Mama with the news and that I planned to come home. I've never received so fast a reply from her." She shuddered. "Mama wrote such awful things. She asked how I could have betrayed the family's honor. How was I to raise the baby on my own with no family support? How would I feel to be at the mercy of every man I met because I would forever be seen as a fallen woman with no scruples?"

Declan froze as she spoke. "She didn't," he whispered. At her nod, his gaze filled with a molten fury, and his hold on her tightened. "Those were her fears and showed her inability to love. They didn't reflect on you."

"How was I to raise a child, Declan? I was alone. Forbidden to ever see my sisters again if I kept my child." She closed her eyes. "However, even that price seemed a price worth paying, as long as I could have Josiah's baby. Keep some small part of him."

"You'll always have him, love. As long as you remember him and the love you shared."

"How can you understand? Why don't you hate me? Condemn me?"

Shaking his head, Declan made a soothing noise. "Never. I could never berate you for what I've also done. Although you had true love and affection between you."

"I didn't do what you did! I gave my baby away!" she cried, as tears coursed out again. "All I had in that miserable place was my good looks and a baby growing in me. I had little money and no one to protect me. The good fortune I had was that of having the support of the doctor's wife. She took me under her wing and gave me a room to sleep in and ensured I never went hungry. She said she knew what it was like to be alone in the world, and she hated to see me suffer."

He paused for a moment, before asking in a quiet murmur, "*Hmm*, are you certain there was no ulterior motive?"

"Oh, there was. I was too naive to see it in the beginning. And, by the time I realized it, I was too dependent on her and her husband's support. And I'd come to realize that I could never raise a child alone. I had no skills. No way of earning money. All the young men were going to war. Even if I had wanted to marry to protect my baby, there was no one I could have married, unless I was willing to marry an old man. And I refused to work in a place like the Bordello. I couldn't. I just couldn't."

"Of course not, love," he whispered.

Her voice broke. "I loved Josiah. I wanted Josiah. I couldn't imagine another man. And then it was obvious I was with child, and no man wanted another man's child."

"Not all men," he whispered.

Lorena stared deeply into his eyes as she nodded. "Not all men." She took a deep breath. "By the time I understood how precarious my situation was, I had few options to help myself. The doctor's wife had been patient and smart. Planting little hints about her childless sister. About the wonderful home she had. About the fact no baby would ever want for anything in such a home."

Declan waited for her to speak before he added in a soft voice, "Except the love of his own mother."

She nodded. "Yes, except for that. But I came to realize I could consign us to a life of hunger and misery and die young. Or I could be selfish and give her up."

"Selfish?" He cupped her face. "How in all that is holy could you ever consider what you did selfish?" His blue eyes gleamed with ardent sincerity. "'Twas the most selfless act any woman could do. To ensure her child was well cared for at the cost of losing her child. A child you cherished and loved and wanted."

"Yes," Lorena whispered, falling forward into his arms again. "I did love my baby and did cherish her. So much." She gripped his shoulders, as though taking strength from his strong arms. "But I gave her up. And I've never spoken about her since. All my sisters were to know was that I'd gone away, suffered a disappointment, and returned. I don't know how Winnifred knew of her."

"How could they not have wondered about what you suffered? You couldn't have returned as the same woman who had left."

"No. I was silent, and I buried myself in books. I barely noticed when Mama picked on Phoebe or when Winnifred pranced around, acting like a brat. I clung to my agony like a shield. For, if I let it go, it meant I would feel again. Be hurt again."

"What happened?" he asked.

Lorena smiled. "The O'Rourkes happened. We traveled here. Phoebe was injured. And your family took us in. For the first time, I was surrounded by a family who loved and cared for each other. That might squabble and fight but wouldn't intentionally hurt each other." She paused and blushed. "I saw what a mother's love was, for the first time."

"Ah, Mum is a special woman," Declan murmured. "We suffered without her."

Lorena gazed into his eyes. "And then you returned, with a baby you claim but who's not yours." She waited for him to lash out at her but saw the quiet acceptance and confirmation in his gaze. "And I was awed at that O'Rourke capacity for love. Hope bloomed that day, and I haven't been able to kill it."

"Don't," Declan pleaded. "Never kill hope. For 'tis the one thing that makes everything we go through bearable." He flushed as he looked at her. "'Twas the hope of you that allowed me to have faith that I'd survive the pain of Magnolia's treachery."

"Of me?" Lorena shook her head. "You didn't know me."

"Of finding a woman like you. Of finding you," Declan said in a reverent tone.

Lorena gazed at him in wonder, her fingers tracing through his beard. Leaning forward, she kissed him, gently and then more firmly, only breaking the kiss when she was gasping for air. "I never dared dream I would meet a man like you. That I could ever deserve a man like you, after what I did."

Shaking his head, Declan ran his fingers through her hair. "No, love, you must change how you see what occurred. Never be ashamed you found a way to ensure your baby thrived. That is a wonderful gift you gave her." He paused. "What did you name her?"

Lorena flushed. "Faith."

He smiled. "A perfect name for her." He sighed as she rested against him. "I love holding you. Feeling you in my arms. Knowing you want to be there."

She squeezed him and pressed closer to him. "Of course I want to be here. I … adore you."

"*Adore*," he murmured. He ran his hands over her back, kissing her head again and again. "What's bothering you, Lo? Something else is festering away inside you." He looked at her, encouraging her to confront what she feared.

She pushed back, her gaze tormented. "I still don't understand how you can stand to look at me. I'm a horrible person. I gave away my child, and now I'm jealous of my own sister's good fortune. I feel envy rather than joy."

He smiled tenderly. "Ah, love, you have it all tangled in your mind again. You're not perfect. I'm not perfect. We feel emotions that bring us shame." He brushed at her hair, as he ran his thumbs over her eyebrows. "Do you think I wasn't desperately envious of my happily married siblings? That I wasn't filled with shame to return home with a baby but no wife?" He shrugged. "I discovered that coming home was the most important thing. Being with family and finding their acceptance as I embraced what I did have. Seeing the love shining in their eyes as they looked at me, understanding they knew how I felt but loved me anyway."

"I've never known that kind of acceptance."

He paused, his fingers stroking over her. "Ah, love, you have, if you only look for it. And I hope you'll be able to find that peace too."

She looked at him, her fingers stroking his stubbled jaw. "I'm starting to." She took a deep breath. "I want to speak with your parents. With the women of your family. I need them to understand."

He shook his head, making soothing noises when her shoulders shrank, and she looked crushed by his words. "No, love, no," he said. "I'm not sayin' you must not speak with them. I simply wish you didn't feel a need to justify yourself or what you've done. You have no need of that. You are remarkable."

"I want them to understand. It's something I have to do, Declan." She stared at his chest.

"Then I'll be by your side—if you want me there. And, if you want to talk with them alone, I'll be waiting impatiently to hold you in my arms to tell you how proud I am of you."

"Oh, my darling," she whispered, snuggling into his embrace once more. "Thank you."

~

Declan sat in the café kitchen, sipping at a cup of tea, while he nibbled on a piece of cake Deirdre had set in front of him. "You know I'll gain a stone if Lorena and I continue to live here."

Deirdre laughed and continued cooking and cleaning up. Her

workday was nearly over, and they could hear Ardan in the café, cajoling the stragglers to leave. However, they both knew it would take him a few more minutes as not many men had anywhere to go, and they enjoyed fine conversations over good cups of coffee.

"Ardan's mastered the art of telling a good tale," Declan said.

Deirdre frowned as she looked at her brother-in-law. "He was always a fine storyteller, Declan. He merely allowed everyone else in the family to shine. Now he has his own place and his own business, with me."

Declan stilled as he considered her words. "I never considered the responsibility he must have felt, as the eldest. And what it was like for him, living in Da's shadow." He paused before whispering, "I envy him."

"There's no need to envy what you yourself have," she said with a wry smile. "You've a wonderful wife, a beautiful son, and you'll soon have employment you find fulfilling."

He stared at her for a long moment. "How do you know that?"

"I know you, and I know O'Rourkes. You'll find a way to make your dreams come true. And your wife's." She smiled at him. "It's in your nature." She squeezed his arm.

Declan took a deep breath, momentarily overcome by strong emotions. Finally he murmured, "You should be at the main house, listening to Lorena's story. She doesn't want to tell her tale more than the one time."

Deirdre shrugged. "I spoke with her for a few moments, before she left. She understood I wouldn't be able to leave." She paused. "I told her of my suspicions." When Declan stared at her with concern, she whispered, "That she lost a child."

Gaping at her, he rasped, "How did you know?"

"I lost one too," she said in a barely audible voice. "Before I moved here. I … My Lydia." She shook her head. "She died. And I never thought I could risk loving again. That I wasn't worthy of loving again." She took a deep trembling breath. "Ardan helped me to see that I was. I am."

"Did she tell you what happened?" Declan asked.

Deirdre nodded, her beautiful eyes filled with sorrow. "I thought death was the worst that could happen, but I wonder now if what Lorena suffered wasn't even more painful." She gripped Declan's hand. "Be patient with her. Her fears will resurface and will take time for her to overcome. But she can overcome them. I promise."

"What can you overcome?" Ardan asked with a frown. "And why are you makin' my wife cry?" he asked in an accusatory tone to his younger brother. He pulled his wife into his side, hugging her close. "Love?" he whispered.

"I'm fine," she murmured into his chest. "I was thinking about Lydia."

"Ah, love," he said, as he held her close and kissed her head. "The café's closed, love, and Declan and I can finish cleaning up down here. Why not rest?"

"Or go spend time with the women of the family?" Declan said.

Deirdre nodded, kissing Ardan on his cheek. "I don't have the opportunity to spend time with them as I'd like. I'll be home soon."

Ardan motioned for Declan to start scrubbing down the counters, as he walked with his wife to his parents' house. Declan washed down the counters and then moved to the stove, polishing it for the next day's work. When Ardan returned, he was sweeping the floor. "Everything all right?"

"We entered at a rather emotional moment, but 'twill be all right. They were delighted at Deirdre's arrival." He moved around the kitchen, putting away pans before nodding with satisfaction that the kitchen was clean. "Come. Da will walk Deir home. Let's have a chat upstairs."

Declan followed his eldest brother upstairs, settling on one of the comfortable chairs in their sitting room. After accepting a small glass of whiskey, he raised it to his brother. "*Sláinte.*" He sighed after taking his first sip.

Ardan sat in a chair facing him, with his long legs stretched out in front of him. "Are you well, Dec?"

Declan sat, matching his eldest brother's relaxed pose, although a tension thrummed through him. "How did you do it?" he asked. When

Ardan stared at him in confusion, he asked, "How did you convince her to trust you? To believe in your love?"

"Ah," Ardan murmured. "Time and constancy." He shrugged. "And she was terrified I was to leave her. To head to Saint Louis. She realized her fear of losing me was greater than her desire to hold onto the pain of the past."

Declan groaned. "I'm not leaving my wife."

Ardan chuckled. "Of course you're not. You'd be daft to. And you'd receive no end of abuse from all of us if you did." He paused. "But you can show your constancy and your love."

Leaning forward, Declan rested his elbows on his knees. "I'm already doing that, but it's not enough."

Sighing, Ardan shook his head. "It takes time, Dec."

"She lost a child," he murmured, sharing a tormented glance with his brother. "She had to give away her baby daughter to be accepted back into her family."

"Ah," Ardan murmured again. "I'd think she'd resent you and all of us." At Declan's quizzical stare, he spoke in a low voice. "You return with a baby, and all we feel is joy at your return. How must that have made her feel?"

Declan rose, pacing around the room, until he came to face the window. "She says she admired us. Envied us."

"Aye, but resentment is a kissin' cousin of envy," Ardan said in a wry tone. "You have to help your lass through all she's feelin'. Those kinds of emotions can bring shame, an' you know as well as I do that we don't like admittin' to them."

Sighing, Declan leaned against the windowsill. "Aye," he said in a soft voice. "I fear she's too used to shrouding herself in a cloak of numbness, so she hasn't had to feel." He looked at his older brother.

"Well, now that she's married an O'Rourke, she won't have that luxury anymore," Ardan said with a wry smile.

Declan chuckled and settled in for a more lighthearted chat with his eldest brother.

∽

Lorena sat in silence, as the women around her stared at her. The only sounds were that of the distant voices of Seamus and his boys, chatting in the living room. Everything in the warm kitchen was silent, even the large stove seemed to understand the solemnity of the moment. Lorena looked from one stunned face to another, hoping to see any hint of understanding. Compassion. Concern. "I beg your pardon," she whispered. "I should never have dared speak of ... of ..."

Phoebe leaped from her chair, yanking her eldest sister into her arms. A sob burst forth as she held her sister, and she clung to her. "Oh, Lo!" she cried out. "I can't believe what you suffered. I can't believe I never knew." She backed away, the tears streaking down her cheeks, as she gazed at her sister with all the love, devotion, and worry Lorena had always dreamed of seeing. "You're so brave. So stoic. I could never have borne such a loss alone." She threw her arms around Lorena again, clinging to her like a burr.

"Forgive me, Phoebe," Lorena whispered. "For being envious of you."

"No, never, no," Phoebe said, finally pushing away to gaze at her sister with intense love. "You have every right, my darling sister." She swiped at her cheeks with the palm of her hand. "My greatest hope is that this won't prevent you from desiring to be aunt to my babe."

"Never," Lorena vowed, her voice cracking. She grunted as Maggie threw herself into her arms, and she held the younger woman tightly to her.

"You're courageous and honorable. You did what you believed you had to do," Maggie said, as she backed away, her brilliant blue eyes brighter, due to the tears she had yet to shed. "Never doubt you are an O'Rourke nor that we're proud to have you in our family."

Tears silently coursed down Lorena's cheeks, as she saw Niamh, Deirdre, and Aileen nod their agreement. She turned to look at Mary, who watched her with a solemn intensity.

"What was your child's name?" Mary asked in a soft voice.

Lorena took a deep breath, nodding in soft acknowledgment to her mother-in-law. "Faith," she whispered.

Mary smiled, as Deirdre stifled a sob and leaned her head against Aileen's shoulder. "Faith," Mary said. "How strong you must have been, to entrust your beautiful babe to another." Mary nodded. "Aye, you had faith."

Lorena shrugged. "I didn't know what else to call her. My heart broke as I handed her ... handed her ..." She shook her head, unable to speak of the moment she gave away her baby. "I failed her," she whispered. "I hoped her name would help her."

"No," Mary said in a strident voice. "You never failed her. You found a way, as too many women have had to do, to find a way." She looked at the women in the room, daughters by blood and by heart, before focusing on Lorena again. "Unlike me, you couldn't find a man to take you on. To tolerate your daughter. Not in the middle of a war." She took a shaky breath. "You found the only solution available to you. Take pride in the fact you protected her."

Lorena lost her battle with tears and fell forward into her mother-in-law's arms. For the first time since she could remember, she felt a mother's love.

∾

Seamus rested in bed, as he watched Mary putter around their small room. Rather than her purposeful movements as she prepared for bed, she paused frequently, easily distracted. "What is it, love?" he murmured, as he watched her uncharacteristic actions.

She jolted and stared at him. "Shay," she breathed, her distant gaze focusing on him. "I was lost to memories for a moment." Crossing to him, she pressed her forehead against his, taking solace from his presence and his constancy.

He wrapped his arms around her, accepting her momentary melancholy, as he attempted to soothe her. "All is well, love."

She rubbed her forehead against his, before collapsing forward into his arms. "The entire time I listened to Lorena speak, about having to give up her wee babe, all I could think about was me. About the horrible days and weeks when Maggie and I were alone and knew we'd starve. Knew we'd freeze to death."

"*Shh*, love, you and Maggie are safe now."

She pushed away to run her fingers through his beard and to look deeply into his eyes. "Tonight I finally realized I had no choice in marrying Francois. 'Tis as though the shame I've carried for so long has been lifted. For Maggie and I would have suffered a fate as severe —or worse—than the one Lorena did." Tears trickled down her cheek. "An' I couldn't have borne that."

"Nay, *a ghrá*," he whispered, his throat tear thickened, as he pulled her tight against him. "My love. You're here with me. And I'm never letting you go."

Mary sobbed quietly into his arms. "I can't imagine having to give up one of my children. 'Twould be like carving away a piece of my heart."

"Oh, love," he breathed, shuddering as he held her tight. "The poor wee lass. 'Tis no wonder she holds herself apart."

"An' why she doubts herself worthy of bein' loved," she whispered.

"Ah, our Declan will help her see the fault in her thinkin'. He'll not be content until there's harmony between them, based on a deep, mutual love."

CHAPTER 14

A few weeks later, Declan slipped into Deirdre's kitchen, where the entire family was eating dinner crammed around her butcher block table. Mum and Maggie needed to help her cook, as the café was busier than usual, so they decided to move their evening meal to the café kitchen, rather attempt to suffer through one of the lads' poorly prepared meals.

Declan frowned upon seeing Winnifred lurking in a corner, glaring at her. She tilted her head up in defiance as she met his harsh stare. "What are you doing here, Winnie?"

"I wanted to see my sisters. I have every right to be at the café." She stared at Deirdre in a challenging manner. "Or is the café barred to me too?"

Deirdre swiped at her forehead, loosening a tendril of red-gold hair, as she studied the defiant younger woman in front of her. "You may stay, for the moment. If you cause trouble, you will be barred."

"I'm not the one who causes problems," Winnifred muttered, as she sat at the corner of the table, gaping in surprise as stools scraped on the wood floor as the nearest O'Rourkes inched away from her.

"Seems not everyone agrees with you," Declan muttered. "Lo?" he asked Deirdre. She nodded upstairs, and he squeezed her arm in thanks, before heading up to find his wife and to urge her down to join his family—their family.

He poked his head into the living room, but it was empty. After a quick knock to their bedroom door, he entered, stilling when he saw her gazing out the back window. "Lo?" he whispered. "Are you well?"

She looked at his reflection in the glass. "As well as I can be."

"What do you mean?" he asked, as he shut the door behind him.

She spun, tripping in her haste to throw herself in his arms. "I feel wrung out. I've needed your arms around me."

He held her close, kissing her head. "Ah, love, all you had to do was ask. Send for me," he whispered, his chest tight with fierce emotions attempting to burst forth. "Had I known you wanted me, I would have dropped everythin' and come to you."

"No," she said in soft voice. "I can't expect you to run to me every time I need you. I must find a way to be strong." She kissed his cloth-covered chest. "But I find I'm stronger when I know I have your support."

"You always have my support, whether or not my arms are around you," he said into her hair. He sighed, easing her away. "Come, love. I have something I have to say, and 'tisn't easy."

She froze, her eyes wide, as she stared at him in fear. "What?" she whispered.

"Love, it's about Winnifred." He waited, as he saw some of her fear abate. "I've been helping to clean up the bookstore. I found somethin' today that made me realize it wasn't an accident."

"What?"

"What is it that Winnifred boasted about to you a few days before the fire?" Declan asked. He saw Lorena shaking her head side to side, as she remained speechless. He caressed her neck. "She went on and on about a locket that your uncle gave her. A locket that she swore she'd never take off." He pulled it from his pocket, covered in soot. "This was near the front door."

"I couldn't get out," Lorena whispered, quivering like an aspen in the fall breeze. "I tried. I pushed and pulled on that door, and I couldn't get out."

He nodded. "Aye. It was somehow already barred."

"She ... I ..." Lorena gasped, short of breath. "I was meant to die?"

Yanking her into his arms, he held her close. "Never. Never, love. If I hadn't looked for you, I know someone else would have noticed the fire." He refused to admit to himself and to her that, had he been any later, she would have perished in the blaze.

She pushed back, her green eyes lit with an unholy fury. "Where is she? Where is my faithless sister who'd see me dead?" She pushed back at her red hair, tying it back in a loose knot. "Take me to where she works."

"There's no need," Declan murmured. "She's downstairs." Muttering under his breath, he followed on her heels, as she raced away from him, her boot heels clattering on the stairs.

Lorena came to a halt in the café kitchen doorway, staring at her sister. After her initial wave of fury washed over her, a deep ache filled her soul. At her sister's betrayal and the loss of all that could have been. She held her hand back, her palm open, waiting until Declan placed the singed locket in her grasp.

When her hand clasped it, she took a deep breath and then moved into the room. Seamus saw her, his storytelling coming to an immediate halt, as he saw the rage and grief in her expression. Suddenly the room was deathly silent, the only sounds those of the diners in the nearby dining room. Lorena marched up to her sister, sitting with empty space to either side of her, as though she were an island or had the plague.

"How could you, Winnie?" Lorena demanded, as she gazed at her sister in horror and betrayal. "How could you?"

Rolling her eyes, Winnifred set down her fork. "Always so dramatic, Lo. Have you been reading too many books again?" She ignored the approach of an irate Declan, who stood behind his wife in silent support.

"No, I've not been reading my books. Have you forgotten that all but a few burned in the recent fire?" She paused. "Or is it that you wish to forget you almost killed your own sister?"

Groaning, Winnifred let out an incredulous snort. "Really, Lo, your imagination has run wild." She jolted with shock as Lorena slammed her hand onto the table.

"I am not delusional. I know the front door, my only escape, was locked, trapping me inside. I know someone threw in a lit torch. *I know*." She paused, as her breath emerged in pants. "What I didn't know until this very moment was that it was you, Winnie. You who planned on killing your own sister." She lifted her hand, revealing the tarnished locket.

Winnifred's eyes widened. "Where'd you find that?"

"In the bookstore's rubble," Declan said, as he glared at his wife's sister. "Right near where the front door used to be." He paused. "Right where you would have stood had you done the vilest act imaginable to your own flesh and blood."

"Lo," Winnifred begged. "You don't understand." Winnifred looked around the table, searching for any sign of understanding or compassion from the gathered O'Rourkes. Instead she saw condemnation and rage. Even Finn, Winnifred's most stalwart champion, looked at her with loathing.

"You're right, Winnie," Lorena said. "I don't understand. I will never understand. You ruined my dream and almost killed me. Do you hate me that much?"

Winnie stood, the stool she'd sat on clattering to the ground. "Of course not! You're my sister." She reached out to touch Lorena, flinching when she jerked away. "I … It was so we could spend more time together. So we could work together with uncle."

With heaving breasts, Lorena gazed at her sister, as though she were a vile stranger. "You ruined my life to force me to work with a cruel man who has no regard for me, who wishes me to become a whore to pay off his debts? You thought you knew what was better for me?" A tear tracked down her cheek. "How could you do such a thing, Winnie?"

"Uncle's in trouble. He's our family."

168

"I'm your family," Lorena roared. "Phoebe's your family. Uncle is nothing! Nothing." She paused, as her breath gasped out of her. "Just as you are now nothing to me. And you never will be again." She turned away, resting against Declan, as she continued to shake.

Winnifred flushed before forcing a look of bravado, as she attempted to explain her way out of her actions. "You were never supposed to have been there, Lo. Only you would work late, worried about where to put dusty books no one wants to read."

"How dare you attempt to turn this into her fault?" Declan rasped, as he held his shaking wife in his arms. "How dare you insinuate your sister was in the wrong for caring so much about her new business that she would spend extra time there?" Declan's blue eyes blazed with hatred and anger. "How dare you?"

"I dare because I know I want more from life!" Winnifred screamed. She looked around at the O'Rourkes, paling at the condemnation and loathing she saw reflected back at her.

Finn stepped forward, placing a warning hand on Declan's shoulder. "What, Win? What more do you want?" When she remained mutinously silent, with her head tilted up and her jaw clamped shut, Finn asked, "What more do you want than a family who would love, honor, and cherish you?" He stared at her with frank devastation in his gaze. "Than a man who would offer you all of that and more?"

"You've never understood."

"Make me!" he roared, his body quivering with his rage. "Make me understand how you can throw this all away," he said in a softer voice, all the more lethal for its restrained rage. "How you can so blithely blame your sister for your folly in nearly killing her. For your lunacy in aligning yourself with your soulless uncle. Have you no shame?"

Winnifred winced, as though his words had finally affected her, but she remained silent.

Seamus cleared his throat, and everyone fell silent, the only sounds in the room harsh breathing and quiet sobs. "Winnifred, I had hoped you'd discover your errors and remedy them. I was wrong." He looked to his wife, who nodded. "Mary was correct in her declaration that you be barred from our home. We should have barred you from our businesses too. However, I believe that is not enough. You must leave Fort Benton. Leave while you still can. For that is the last bit of mercy any of us will show you now."

"Leave?" Winnifred gasped. "I … I have nothing and no one anywhere else." She looked to Finn with pleading and desperation. "Please."

"Leave, Win," Finn said. "There's nothing and no one here for you. Not anymore. Accept the last drop of aid my family will give you and don't look back." He stepped away to align himself with the wall of O'Rourkes facing Winnifred, ignoring her sobs and her outstretched palms, begging him for succor. He stared at her dispassionately, as he watched her race from the café kitchen.

Declan held onto Lorena, when she would have slipped free of his embrace. "No, love, no," he whispered. "You're not alone, and you'll never be alone. You're my wife. You're an O'Rourke." He kissed her on the side of her neck. "You're so much more but now's not the time."

Declan watched as his brother Finn's heart broke while Lorena quietly wept against his chest at the loss of her youngest sister, as her family shattered apart. Declan knew he'd never be able to mend either loss.

That evening Lorena slipped from the bed she shared with Declan, moving to stare out the window overlooking the back of the town. For once, she wished their room overlooked the front, as she yearned for at least one more sighting of her youngest sister. With a sigh, she rested her head against the cool windowpane, as the curtain fluttered around her.

Holding one hand to her heart, Lorena knew she needed to mourn her sister. To let her go. For the adult Winnifred had never shown her familial love. She had only ever shown disdain and an utter disregard for Lorena's needs. However, Lorena could not fight grieving the memory of the little sister she had known. Before age and the need to impress had altered her baby sister. Before the fear of poverty and her lost faith in love had warped Winnifred's priorities.

Rather than the heartless woman who had attempted to brazen her way out of nearly killing Lorena after ruining Lorena's precious bookstore, Lorena saw the little girl who played hide-and-seek with her in the back garden. Rather than the vindictive woman who ruthlessly spoke about Lorena's past in an attempt to humiliate and to shame Lorena, Lorena saw a tiny imp with black curly hair, playing at a tea party.

"You look like a spirit," Declan murmured.

She shrieked, spinning to face him, and entangled herself in the curtain. At his chuckle, she attempted a smile, but a deep sob burst forth.

"Oh, love," Declan soothed, as he vaulted out of bed and eased her into his arms. "I should have left you to think. Forgive me."

"No," she whispered, as she pressed against his chest, her voice cracking with her panic. "No, I don't want to be alone. Please, don't leave me alone."

He gripped her tight. "Ah, love," he whispered into her ear, his hands rubbing over her back, and he felt her muscles ease as she relaxed fully against him. "You're not alone. I'll never leave you alone. I promise."

Tears leaked out, and she rubbed her face against his chest. "I've always felt alone, even in a crowded room." She sniffled. "Even in your family's crowded kitchen, with everyone chattering away, I always felt apart. As though I would never belong. Never to be part of the chaos."

Declan made soothing noises, easing her back so he could look into her eyes, his thumbs stroking gently over her soft cheeks. "'Tis a shame, Lo," he said with a soft smile. "For I know how cherished you are by my family. My mum considers you her daughter. Maggie and Niamh are delighted to have another sister, as are the lads."

Her lower lip quivered, until she bit it with her teeth. She gazed deeply into his somber, sincere blue eyes, ignoring the tears pooling and dropping from hers to course down her cheeks. "I ... I didn't know how to accept such love."

"No," her husband said in a soft chiding tone, "you believed your-self unworthy. Something I've felt too often myself."

Lorena stared at him with undisguised agony in her gaze. "My own sister tried to kill me." At his quiet nod, a sob burst forth. "Win-nifred tried to kill me." Her voice stuttered over the last two words, as she relaxed into his embrace.

"I'm sorry, love. I'm so sorry I was the one to discover the truth," he whispered into her ear, as he held her while she sobbed.

"I'm not," she said against his neck. "I'm so thankful it was you. That the truth didn't remain hidden. That we discovered the truth and that I was forced to finally face the extent of her betrayal." She arched back to meet his gaze, frowning when she saw the depth of concern in his gaze. "That it was you who told me."

"Why?"

"Was it hard for you to tell me?" At the jerk of his head indicating it was, she smiled and cupped his face. "Did it hurt you to know the pain it would cause me?"

"You know it did, Lo," he whispered, his eyes shining with sincerity.

"And yet you didn't falter. You still told me. With concern and caring of utmost importance." She smiled at him. "I've been so afraid of trusting you, for fear of having that trust prove me a fool." She shook her head and sniffled, her eyes glowing with pride as she gazed at him. "I realize I have no reason to doubt you. You are honorable and trustworthy and beloved."

"Oh, Lo," Declan breathed as he pulled her close, his arms squeezing her tight. "I feared you'd blame me. Resent me for discov-ering the truth, for being the message bearer."

"Never," she said, kissing the side of his throat.

He whispered into her ear, "I know what it is to be betrayed by a beloved sibling. And to learn to forgive."

She jerked back in confusion. "What do you mean?"

He smiled, tracing her jaw with his thumb. "No one ever tried to kill me. 'Twasn't anything that dramatic. But Kevin stole my bride. Met her on her trip up the Missouri. And let me court her, while he loved her the whole time and dreamed of her. And she dreamed of him. Never of me. Can you imagine what a fool I felt?" He shook his head, closing his eyes. "And to know Ardan was aware and never thought to tell me either."

"What did you do?" she whispered, kissing the underside of his jaw.

"We yelled. Had a fight in the Sunrise." He shrugged as she gaped at him openmouthed. "Men need to fight sometimes, love. And, no matter what Kev says, I won that fight." At her loyal nod of agreement, he grinned at her. "And then we had Aileen choose. She chose me, but only because her aunt was blackmailing her. Thankfully Mum spoke up at our weddin', stopping the ceremony."

"Oh my," Lorena whispered.

"Aye, more reason to be mortified, watching my bride race away from me, with the whole town watchin'." He shrugged, as though it had never bothered him.

"I'm sorry you were prevented from marrying her," Lorena whispered.

He gave of huff of incredulity and then chuckled. "I'm not. Kev and Aileen are gloriously content. And I wasn't meant to be with her. She would never have cared for me as she loves Kevin. And Kevin would have been miserable." He stared away for a moment. "He would have left. Split the family. And everyone would have been unhappy. Not just the three of us."

"How long did it take you to forgive him?" she whispered.

"A part of me forgave immediately. They were happy in a way I thought I'd never understand." He stilled as he shared a long look with her. "But a deeper part, the part of me that yearned for marriage and love and companionship, was bitter. And determined that I was as good as any of my brothers. That I would be found as worthy."

She cupped his face. "You are, Declan. How can you doubt?" She kissed him, wrapping her arms around his neck.

"Oh, how I cherish you, lass," he breathed into her ear.

Kissing his jaw, she whispered, "Take me to bed, husband. Show me how much you cherish me."

He swooped down, kissing her passionately. "With the greatest pleasure, my love."

~

A weak breeze blew, unable to clear the air of the mild stench of a town bursting with more people than it was ever meant to hold. The smell of woodsmoke, horse dung, refuse, and pungent men mingled together to create a noxious perfume. Hot summer days only added to the fetid smell, although soon the steamboats would all be at Cow Island, and there would be fewer men in town. Declan was looking forward to that day, although he knew it signaled the beginning of the slow season for the family businesses.

A week had passed since the fight with Winnifred in Deirdre's kitchen. Lorena had continued to stoically work with her sister-in-law, although each day she was a little more withdrawn. A little more softly spoken. Declan yearned for the fiery woman who had confronted Winnifred. He yearned for her to never know the agony of a sibling's betrayal.

Today Declan stood beside Lorena on the levee's edge, watching as passengers boarded a steamboat headed back to Saint Louis. Crew hauled on crates of pelts, while miners cast furtive glances at those near them, as they carried their precious metals back with them.

"Do you think they all struck it rich?" Finn asked, as he sidled up beside Declan and Lorena. He nodded his hello at Lorena. "So many of them act as though they hit the mother lode, when they most likely just discovered enough to pay their fare home."

Declan shrugged, keeping his arm around Lorena's waist. "Well, however much they found, 'tis important enough to make them cautious." His gaze focused on one man with sandy-blond hair and a hooked nose. "He seems the cagiest."

Finn tilted his head to the side as he studied him. "Aye." With a shake of his head, he focused on his brother and sister-in-law. "Has she arrived yet?" When they shook their heads, he sighed. "Don't know why I even bothered to come today. We're busy enough at the store."

"You know why you came," Lorena whispered. "You mourn her leaving but need to reassure yourself that she actually departs." She stared deeply into his tear-brightened blue eyes, reaching out to grip his arm.

"How typical," Winnifred hissed, as she sauntered up to them. "You're not satisfied with one man, so now you're trying for two."

Lorena stiffened at the snide words, her hand dropping from Finn's arm, as she leaned into her husband's embrace. "Winnie," Lorena said, her voice breaking. She cleared her throat, speaking in a stronger tone. "I wish you'd allow us to take leave of each other under better terms. Without a forced bitterness between us."

"There's nothing forced about it," her youngest sister said with a flounce of her curly black hair. She jutted out one hip, smiling when she saw men lingering near the ship focus on her womanly curves. "We've never been close."

Scenes from their youth flashed through Lorena's mind, and she shook her head. "You know that's not true, but you're the one who has to live with your own life's disappointments." She stood tall as she faced her sister. "I wish you well. I hope you find whatever it is you seek."

For a long moment, the sisters shared an unguarded gaze, Lorena's filled with resigned disappointment, while Winnifred was unable to hide the terror and uncertainty in hers. Finally Lorena took a deep breath and whispered, "Godspeed, Winnie."

Winnifred looked from Lorena to Finn, before spinning on her heel and racing toward the steamboat. Finn took a step after her, before catching himself and forcing himself to freeze.

"Finn," Declan murmured.

"No," Finn rasped. "You can go if you want. I'll wait and make sure she leaves."

Lorena squeezed her brother-in-law's arm one more time, before departing without a backward glance.

~

Later that evening, the café had closed, and Dierdre and Ardan had retired upstairs. Lorena promised to clean up the kitchen and await Declan's return. She looked up from washing dishes to see her sister Phoebe, hovering in the rear doorway. Dropping the dish into sudsy water, she scrubbed her wet hands on her apron, nearly tripping in her haste to reach her ashen sister. "Phoebe!" she gasped, as her hands clasped her sister's shoulders. "Are you all right?" She pushed her to a stool and hovered over her. "The baby?"

Phoebe reached out a quivering hand, her head shaking. When Lorena paled, Phoebe gasped, "No!" She held on to Lorena's hand. "No, I'm fine. The baby is fine. I think." Her brows furrowed. "I'm not sure how I'm supposed to know." She looked to her sister hopefully.

Lorena ran a soothing hand over her sister's head. "Have you felt a fluttering in your belly yet? Like little butterfly wings trying to break free?" At Phoebe's gasp and nod, Lorena smiled. "That's when you know your baby is well. Soon you'll feel more movement, and then you'll wish the little creature would calm and give you time to rest." She gazed with fondness at her sister.

"I'm sorry, Lo," Phoebe whispered, her eyes filled with sorrow. "I wish I'd known. I wish I could have helped you. And I'm sorry ..." She paused and shook her head. "I'm *not* sorry I'm having this baby, for I already love it so much, but I'm worried you'll leave me again. Disappear into your books."

Tears trickled down Lorena's cheeks. "Never." She swiped at her face and forced a smile. "I'll always wish our children could have grown up together. Become great friends. But I'll relish being an aunt." She bit her lip. "And hopefully, someday soon, you'll be an aunt for one of my children."

Phoebe gaped at her. "You're willing to try again?" She flushed. "I know it's unseemly to talk of such things."

Lorena squeezed her arm. "Not unseemly. A little embarrassing perhaps. But I've found myself dreaming of holding a child that has Declan's black hair and my green eyes. And the sorrow doesn't over-

176

whelm me. I've found hope again, Phoebe." Her eyes filled. "And it's almost more terrifying than love." Her jaw quivered at her admission, as she met her sister's compassionate stare.

Phoebe opened her arms, pulling her close. "It is. But, when the promise of that hope is fulfilled, it's glorious, Lo. Have faith."

"I'm trying to," Lorena said. She sighed, enjoying the closeness with her sister.

"We lost one of us today," Phoebe whispered, her voice tear thickened.

Lorena nodded her head against her sister's shoulder. "I know. I went to the steamboat to say goodbye. And to ensure she left." She eased away, battling shame at her sense of relief that her youngest, most meddlesome sister was on her way downriver. "I couldn't ..." She broke off. "I knew I wouldn't build the life I wanted here if she were to remain. Somehow she'd sully what I'm building with Declan. Something vile she would say would take root and would bloom between us, causing a distance we'd find hard to overcome due to her deceit."

"Duty says I should have gone. I should have seen her off." Phoebe sat here with a distant look in her eye. Finally she focused on her eldest sister. "But I couldn't. Not after how she's treated us. She attempted to ruin my marriage. She tried to kill you." Her eyes blazed with anger. "I fear I'll never forgive her, and I worried at what I would have said. I know she wanted sympathy as she left. All I felt was joy. And I knew I'd gloat."

Lorena nodded. "No matter what you believe, Phoebe, I know you would have felt sorrow. She was terrified. And devastated Finn wouldn't save her at the last minute." Lorena shook her head ruefully. "I think she believed he'd speak up, ask her to stay."

"Marry him?" Phoebe said, with an incredulous snort and roll of her eyes. "Finn wouldn't go against his parents, and he's been as disappointed as any O'Rourke at how she's acted."

"Perhaps more so," Lorena murmured. "He wanted to believe her. Kept giving her time to redeem herself and second chances she never deserved. And, in the end, he couldn't tolerate her deception any longer." She sighed before whispering a deeply held fear. "I still worry Declan will come to believe in the vile things she said about me."

Phoebe tilted her head to one side, as she studied her eldest sister. "Eamon believed me. Believed *in* me, not Winnifred. You must trust Declan will do the same for you."

Lorena's eyes filled. "You didn't have the same ... secrets as I did. As what I did—" She closed her eyes in agony. "How can he trust in my steadfastness? In my loyalty to him and Gavin and to any other children we may have?"

Phoebe's jaw set, as she stared at her sister with concern. "Because he loves you." At the flare of panic mixed with hope in her sister's eyes, Phoebe smiled with compassion and understanding.

"Love didn't keep Josiah from leaving. Love didn't keep Josiah from dying. Love didn't save my child from being given away." She paced the small space in the kitchen near the sink and back to her sister. "Love is never enough."

Phoebe nodded, rising from her stool to stand in front of her sister, so Lorena had to cease walking back and forth. "Perhaps you're right. Perhaps love isn't strong enough to prevent horrible things from happening. But, without it, life is barren. Can you imagine living these past years without the memory of Josiah's love for you? Or the love you have for your babe? Can you imagine living now without the love of the O'Rourke family? Or without seeing Declan's adoration for you in his gaze? Your life would be empty, Lo, without all the love shown to you every day."

"It's only adoration. It's not love," Lorena said with a defiant tilt of her chin, as she referred to her husband and ignored everything else Phoebe had said.

"Will you ever believe in his love for you? Or must he spend his whole life trying to prove it to you?" Phoebe asked in a soft voice. "For, if you doubt and doubt, his love for you will decay and will become a fragment of what he felt for you, mingled with resentment and duty. And you will have lost your chance to experience unfettered joy again."

Lorena watched as her sister walked out the back door, her words ringing in the otherwise silent room.

~

Declan worried that Ardan and Deirdre would tire of having guests, but Ardan seemed delighted that their large home was serving its purpose. Gavin usually woke once in the middle of the night, but he rarely cried and was generally a cheery child. Declan couldn't believe his son would soon be one year old.

This morning Lorena rested on her side staring into space, her long beautiful hair cascading down her back, free of any braids. "Lorena, love, why are you hiding yourself away?" Declan asked, as he stood just inside their bedroom door.

"Why do you use endearments with me?" she asked, as she continued to stare at a space on the wall opposite her. "Why pretend?"

"Pretend?" he asked, coming to kneel beside the bed and to block her view of the far wall. He frowned as he saw the desolation in her gaze. "What's happened, my love?"

She pushed herself up, her hair shimmering around her shoulders. "There. Right there. You call me your love. Do you mean it?" she asked. "Or is it all something you say that means nothing?"

"Of course I mean it." He took a deep breath to calm his roiling emotions and to prevent himself from saying something that could bring her pain. "You haven't been ready to hear it."

"I'm that much of a weakling?"

He gripped her hand, his jaw clenching and unclenching. "No. You're the bravest, strongest woman I know. And I know quite a few strong women," he said, alluding to his mum, Maggie, and Niamh. "I worried you'd find a reason to leave, if you knew how much I felt. Find a way to distance yourself from me."

She shook her head. "How can you care for me when my own sister tried to kill me? My own mother forced me to make an impossible choice!" She took a deep gulping breath. "There's something wrong with me, Declan." She held a hand to her chest. "I'm not worthy of … of …"

"Love?" he said in a confident voice. "For I love you, Lorena. I love you like I never knew it was possible to love. With every part of me. And I will do everything in my power to protect you."

Her eyes rounded, as she stared at him in awe. "You can't," she breathed, shaking her head.

His cheeks flushed red, and his nostrils flared, as he took a deep breath. "Don't tell me what I can and cannot feel, Lo."

She sat in stunned silence for a long moment. "My name," she murmured, as she continued to stare at him in wonder. "You've always said it in a way to make it sound as though it were the sweetest endearment."

Letting out a pent-up breath, he nodded. "I don't remember the Gaelic, like Da and a few of my siblings do." His eyes glowed with the fervency of his emotions. "'Twas a way I could show you how much I cared without declaring it to the world. Or you."

"I'm a fool," she whispered. She gasped as Declan rose, striding for the door and slamming it shut behind him. "No," she breathed, as she watched him run away from her. "No, wait."

Holding a hand to her racing heart, Lorena sat in stunned silence as she realized her every dream was within her grasp. If only she had the courage to reach for it.

CHAPTER 15

A few weeks later, Fort Benton was now welcoming men from the mining towns, wishing to return to the larger cities. They spent a few days or a week in Fort Benton, before hitching a ride to Cow Island and a waiting steamboat. Although the café remained busy, there wasn't nearly as much commerce in the family store, and the warehouse was no longer a hive of activity.

Since the night he had declared his love and had been rebuffed, Declan had not spent more than a few moments in his wife's presence. He had snubbed her every overture to talk and had slept away from Ardan's. He took his meals with his family and sat beside her as a dutiful husband, but he did not laugh or join in the conversations. He refused to hold her hand. Or gaze at her like the lovesick idiot he was.

Instead he focused on a project that he had begun before their argument. One that he now worked on like a man possessed. For he believed, if he could just finish it, he could prove his love. Could earn it and be worthy of it.

As the hot afternoon sun burned down on them, his brother Kevin swiped at his forehead, a hammer in his hand and a nail in the corner of his mouth, as he tried to talk to his brother. "You'll have to talk to her again at some point, Dec. She *is* your wife." He looked around them. "You'll have to tell her about what you've been doing."

"I'm not tellin' her anything until I've finished," Declan said with a defiant tilt of his head. His hair was longer, and his beard hadn't been trimmed in days, if not weeks.

Niall heaved out a breath, as he paused his work and took a long sip of water, before mimicking his older brothers and swiping at his forehead with the back of his forearm. "If you don't tell her somethin' soon, she'll leave. She already thinks you've found another."

"What?" Declan demanded. "She can't be that daft. I told her that I loved her."

"Aye, an' ran away two minutes later. You never gave your lass a chance to believe you." Kevin shook his head, before moving away to keep working. "Stop reacting out of fear, Dec."

Declan huffed out an aggrieved breath, as he turned toward a wall and hammered in a nail so hard he nearly splintered the board. His mind raced at the possibility she now doubted him. After moments of anger, where he indignantly replayed all the times he had been good to her, he rested his forehead against one of the planks.

His mad desire to finish this project, to prove to her that he loved her, now seemed pointless. An unutterable sadness and sense of futility filled him, and he wanted to bawl like a baby. Instead he pushed back and focused on the task at hand. Looking around, he knew they had a few more weeks' worth of work. He wondered if he would still have a marriage worth salvaging at that point.

That evening, Declan sat beside Lorena, although his attention was on his father, who seemed distracted. Mum had baked a cake, and they planned to celebrate Gavin's birthday tonight. Thus the table was crowded as everyone was present, including Niamh, Cormac, and their children. He glanced to the door to see Dunmore standing there, his hat in his hands, as his gaze tracked Maggie's every move with a devout attentiveness. Declan's gaze rose to meet his father's, and Seamus nodded once. Suddenly Declan knew his son's birthday dinner was an excuse to have everyone gather, so as to discuss the real concern facing the family.

"Oh no," Declan murmured. He instinctively reached for Lorena's hand, freezing when she stiffened at his action. "I beg your pardon," he whispered, as he released her hand, as though it were on fire. Gripping his thigh, he clenched his jaw at her persistent rejection and at his ongoing hope that things would change.

"Da," Niamh asked with a smile. "Why were you insistent we all come to dinner? There's barely room for all of us." She frowned as A.J. entered with a wide grin and a wink to Maggie and Mary.

"We always make room for friends," Seamus said in a voice that brooked no argument. "And we should celebrate wee Gavin's birthday."

Niamh demurred, Cormac whispering in her ear.

Soon they were all seated, with A.J. near Seamus and Mary, and Dunmore sitting across from Maggie. At the knock on the back door, Bryan hopped up. "I'll get it, although they'll have to sit on the floor!" He flung the door open, his eyes widening. "I'll sit on the floor," he stammered out. "You're very welcome."

Mary smiled at Madam Nora, rising to run a hand down Bryan's back. "Sit, love," she murmured in Bryan's ear, watching with a wry quirk of her lips as he scurried away, his green eyes wide as he stared at the Bordello owner. He was just about old enough to understand what the Siren's profession meant.

"Nora," Mary said, "come join us as we celebrate Gavin's birthday and say Godspeed to Mr. Pickens and pray for his return next season."

With a careful glance in Seamus's direction, Nora smiled. "Thank you. I always enjoy any reason to gather with the O'Rourke family."

Mary turned to stare at her husband but merely nodded. "There's never enough chance to celebrate, and there's always too much work. As wee Bryan said, you're very welcome."

"I'm not so wee," Bryan muttered as he stared at his nephews. "Gavin and Cillian are younger."

"Aye, that they are, my lad," Seamus said. "And not nearly as handsome." He chuckled as Bryan brightened at his comment. After room had been made for everyone present, Seamus said grace and plates were filled. After a hearty, simple dinner, Seamus motioned for everyone to remain seated. "We'll have cake after our discussion."

Declan tensed, calming only when Lorena shifted ever-so-slightly in his direction. "Da, do you want me to start?" At his father's terse nod, Declan looked in Maggie's direction. "Mags, I'd never want you to worry."

Maggie tensed, her easy teasing smile as she whispered secrets to Dunmore coming to an abrupt halt. "Worry?" she asked, as she looked around the table. "This isn't a party at all, is it?"

Shaking his head, Declan tucked a strand of hair behind his ear, although it wasn't yet long enough that it remained there for longer than a few seconds. "I've heard from A.J. and from Madam Nora that Jacques's interest in you has not abated."

Maggie froze, staring at them in horror. "Jacques?" she whispered. "I thought he'd forgotten about me."

"No, Miss Maggie," Dunmore said in his slow drawl. "He hasn't." When she stared at him in betrayal, he reached across the table to clasp her hand. "No, sweetheart," he murmured. "I've tried to keep an ear to the ground for his whereabouts. I discovered earlier this summer that he's been in a small mining town south of Helena for the past year. But he's up and disappeared again. I worry he's on his way back here."

"But why?" Maggie asked, flushed and nearly out of breath as she fought panic. She sat with stooped shoulders, as though attempting to become invisible.

"Now, my darlin' girl," Seamus said, "you know every one of us here will protect you." He looked around the table as a chorus of "Ayes" sounded at his pronouncement. "But it means you must never wander alone. Not until we know what he has planned."

Maggie looked to her father and then to Dunmore. "Tell me what you know." When they shared a long look and appeared reluctant to say anything more, she firmed her jaw and looked down the table to the Madam. "Nora? Please."

Nora cleared her throat and sat with impeccable posture, as she ignored the warning glance Seamus sent her. "What I have heard is only hearsay, Maggie. Thirdhand at best," she murmured. "But I find that relaxed men tend to reveal more than they'd like." When A.J. made a grunt of agreement, she smiled. "From what I've been able to piece together from bits of conversation, Jacques plans to return and to steal you away from your family. He doesn't want you to be with anyone but him."

At the deafening silence, A.J. spoke. "Aye, that's what I've heard too. And that he's in cahoots with that puffed-up peacock, Chaffee." He smiled apologetically at Lorena and Phoebe. "Watch yourselves around him too."

"Oh, uncle," Lorena whispered mournfully.

Declan yearned to wrap an arm around her shoulder but feared his sign of compassion would be rebuffed again. Instead he fisted and unfisted his hand on his lap, wishing he could touch his own wife. "I worry they won't remain focused only on Maggie," Declan said. "Chaffee's in debt and becoming desperate. There's no telling what a man will do when he's backed into a corner."

Seamus nodded. "Aye," he said. "From now on, we all travel in groups. Except for the eldest lads." He shook his head when the youngest boys began to protest. "And, when we have news, we share it. With all." He relaxed when Nora nodded. "Now 'tis time for cake and to celebrate wee Gavin. And to mourn the imminent departure of A.J. I can only hope you have the sense to return to us again next year, for you'll be sorely missed, Captain."

A.J. smiled at them. "Well, I have to talk it over with my Bessie, but I suspect you'll be seein' me again."

A few days later, Seamus approached the worksite with a glower and an irate gleam in his eyes. "Lads," he said to his sons, working on the opposite side of the building from Declan. "Go visit your mum or Deirdre and have a long lunch." He watched as Kevin and Niall set down their tools and scurried away.

Approaching Declan, Seamus let out a sigh. "Do you really believe this will prove anything, lad?"

"Da," Declan said, as he spun to face his father. He strode to the water pail, scooped out a handful of water to rub over his face and another for his neck, and then took a sip. Finally he looked at his da again. "What brings you here?"

"I had thought my scholarly son had more brains than a woodpecker, but I can see I was mistaken." Seamus stood at his full height, his salt-and-pepper hair blowing in the soft breeze.

"Da, you don't understand," Declan protested. When Da made a warning sound, and his glower intensified, Declan bit back what more he would have said.

"Don't tell me I don't understand when my lad's gone mad," he snapped. "Do you think by buildin' this"—he waved around at the framed structure—"that you'll prove you love her? That you'll be worthy of her love?" Seamus shook his head. "You know as well as I do that it doesn't work that way."

"Da," Declan murmured, swallowing as he suddenly fought tears. "I told her that I loved her. I've shown her I love her in every way I can." His blue eyes, eyes that matched his father's, shone with desperation. "I have to try."

Seamus strode the few paces to his son, gripping his shoulders. "Talk to your wife, Declan. She's miserable. Nearly as miserable as you are."

Closing his eyes, Declan whispered, "I told her that I loved her, Da, and she called me a fool." He looked at his father. "I thought she was different."

Seamus hauled him close, wrapping his son in strong arms that had never wavered in his love for him. "Ah, lad, there has to be some misunderstandin'. Something isn't right in what you say. Either you misheard her or she misspoke." He leaned back, gazing into his son's eyes. "What you're buildin' is a tribute to the love you have for her, aye. But you should be sharin' this with her. Gettin' her opinions and sharin' the excitement with her. 'Tis half the fun." He paused. "An' you have to find a wee bit more courage and face her, Dec. Face her as you truly are, not as you believe she wants you to be."

Taking a deep breath, Declan nodded. "Aye. Tonight."

Lorena worked in the café kitchen, now not nearly as busy as in July, but still with a steady stream of customers. She knew that soon the café would reduce its hours and would offer only one meal a day. However, for now, Ardan and Deirdre were capitalizing on the presence of the numerous men who would never be residents. With a wry smile, Lorena knew she should learn as much as she could from Ardan and Deirdre about running a successful business. Lorena's smile dimmed, as she doubted she'd ever have a business to run.

"Why the glower, Lorena?" Deirdre asked, as she paused in measuring out ingredients for a batch of cinnamon rolls, which she would leave to rise overnight.

Lorena grimaced, as she hadn't realized Deirdre was paying her any attention. "Oh, I couldn't help but think about my store again. And wish that my own sister hadn't brought about its destruction."

Deirdre watched her with patient understanding. "I can't imagine the heartache you suffered." She looked around at her kitchen. "Even though I know I could rebuild as long as I had Ardan, it takes time to come to terms with the magnitude of your loss." She paused. "I fear our family can become focused on rebuilding and not understand that it is necessary to have the time to mourn."

"Do you believe that?" Lorena asked. "I thought they were considerate of me when I told them my tale and appreciated I needed to mourn."

Deirdre sighed and rubbed at her head, smearing her forehead with flour. "That's not what I mean. The men mourn, in their own way, but they also fear loss. All of them, in their own way, suffered at the loss of Mary and Maggie, and with the stepmother. They honor mourning, but I know they shy away from an excess of emotion to hide their vulnerability."

"Don't we all?" Lorena asked with a wry smile. She stared at the gentle compassion in Deirdre's gaze before blurting out, "Declan doesn't love me anymore."

Unable to stifle an incredulous laugh, Deirdre shook her head. "You've never been more wrong. The man's mad for you." She bit her lip. "Plans are afoot, and I can't speak of them without betraying him." She paused again. "What do you know to be true, Lorena? Before everything went wrong between you, what was true?"

"He loved me," she whispered. "I know he did. No man would treat me as he did if he didn't love me." Lorena dried her hands and then repinned her red hair into a bun. "I loved him too, but I was never able to tell him." Suddenly she fought an onslaught of tears. "I wonder if it wouldn't be better all-around if I just simply leave. I can't imagine it brings him any joy to suffer through family dinners, seated beside me."

"Don't leave, Lorena. Whatever you do, promise me that you won't leave." She paused until Lorena nodded her agreement. "You know that feeling you described, of feeling precious to him?" When Lorena gave a subtle nod, Deirdre beamed at her, holding a hand to her heart, uncaring that she smeared dough on her apron. "Hold that feeling here, Lorena, and don't allow it to burn out. For I know O'Rourke men, and I know he'll find a way to reconcile with you. Don't doubt him."

Lorena forced a smiled and turned back to the pan of dishes, her mind filled with imaginings of a harmonious life with Declan. Although she tried to cling to the hope Deirdre attempted to impart, Lorena knew it was fleeting and that, too soon, she would find herself alone in her bed again, dreaming of feeling safe and cherished in her husband's arms. How she wished it were all more than a dream.

Lorena sat on a bench she had placed by the back window, staring at the clouds changing color as evening slowly arrived. She loved the long twilights here. The way the clouds had a tinge of pink on their undersides, as the sun had one last gasp of brilliance before falling over the horizon. Hugging her knees to her chest, she wondered if that was all she and Declan would have. One tiny bit of brilliance before the bitterness and distrust ruined all they were trying to create.

Anger, disbelief, and hurt filled her as she considered the past weeks. Although she tried to stay busy working in Deirdre's kitchen, she was unable to avoid Declan completely. And, if she were honest with herself, she longed for the glimpses of him she had. She yearned to squeeze his hand, to lean into him at the kitchen table, to tease him about his ever-longer hair and untamed beard. Instead she sat with a remote sullenness, as though his presence was distasteful.

A tear coursed down her cheek, as she remembered the early days of her marriage. Of the joyful glint in his eyes every time he saw her. Of his solicitude. His almost desperate need to ensure she was well. Now she wondered if he would notice if she left.

She had mentioned to Deirdre the possibility of leaving, but Lorena knew in her heart that she didn't want to. She wanted to remain here, with her husband. If only he wanted her too. Letting out a deep sigh, she tugged her knees even closer to herself and rocked a little bit, wishing his arms were around her. She closed her eyes, imagining the sensation of being in his arms again. Of breathing in his musky scent again. "Oh, Declan," she whispered.

"What, lass?" he whispered, so near she felt his breath on her temple.

Shrieking, she spun and gaped at him. "Declan!" she gasped, holding a hand to her heart, as she attempted to catch her breath. "What are you doing here?"

He knelt by the bench, his blue eyes intense in the fading daylight. "My wife is here. I've spent too much time away from her."

With her eyes filling with tears, she asked in a tear-choked voice, "I thought you'd found another. That you ..." She shook her head, unable to speak the words.

"Never," he growled, as though she had spoken a blasphemy. "Never, my love. How can you think me so fickle?"

Her eyes widened, and the shock and joy of his appearance transmuted into fury. "How could I not?" She tapped him on his shoulder. "You ignore me. You won't touch me. You refuse to spend a moment in my company, unless you're at your parents' house for a meal. I doubt you've thought of me at all since that day."

His blue eyes lit with indignation. "I haven't thought of you at all?" he bellowed. He rose, gripping her hand. "Come with me." After ensuring she had shoes on, he tugged her down the stairs, out the back door, and across a field. "Watch for gopher holes, love," he murmured, steering her clear of a few places where she would have twisted an ankle. When she shivered in the cooling night air, he shrugged out of his jacket and placed it over her. Soon he paused his mad dash away from town and stopped.

Lorena held a hand on her hip as she gaped at a half-completed building. "I don't understand what this is."

He waved at her. "Your new store."

Her eyes widened, and she held a hand to her mouth. "No. You can't. It's too much," she stammered out, as she unconsciously walked toward it. "Can I go inside?" she asked with a childlike delight, as she was unable to hide her glee.

He smiled at her joy. "Of course. Let me show you what I envision." He gripped her hand and helped her inside. "This would be the main area, where you'd showcase and sell your books. We'll brick this part of the wall for the potbellied stove," he said, as he motioned to a sidewall near the back. "That way, you'll always be warm, even when you sell books in the middle of winter."

With a gentle tug, he pulled her through a doorframe. "This is my space," he said. "Where I'll tutor children from town."

"Oh, Declan, what a brilliant idea. You have so much to share with the children here." She beamed at him, her smile fading, as she looked deeply into his eyes. "The walls seem taller than we need them to be."

He grinned at her. "'Tis because we'll have two stories. We'll live upstairs."

"Oh, how perfect," she said, with a contented sigh, before frowning. "I have no books. I have no reason for a store."

"Ah, 'tisn't true," he murmured, as he rubbed at his neck. "I was helpin' to clean up the warehouse after our argument ..." He paused, flushing at the memory. "And I found crates of books that had been overlooked. Seems they came in a later shipment, and Niall never mentioned them to me."

"I have more books?" she asked with excitement.

"Aye, not nearly as many as before but some. Enough for a start." He grunted, as she threw herself into his arms. With a sigh, he wrapped his arms around her, breathing in deeply of her scent. "God, I've missed you, lass."

She pushed away, shaking her head, as she stared at him with hurt and hope fighting for supremacy. "Why do you believe this is enough?" she asked, waving her arm around at the building site.

He patted at his head and then at his beard. "I'm sorry I didn't shave and see the barber."

"No, Declan," she said, her gaze filled with confusion. "I don't care what you look like. I don't care if you have hair so long I could tie it into a braid. Or a beard I could braid." She smiled with a tender sadness. "Why did you run from me? Why have you been so cold?" When he stared at her in strained silence, she asked in a broken voice, "Did you even mean it?"

He yanked her to him, his fingers digging into her hair, as he held her so tightly she couldn't move. "Of course I meant it. I love you." He paused a moment as he stared into her eyes, waiting for her to say something. Finally, he whispered, "You called me a fool."

Her expression softened, as she relaxed under his tight grip. "No, Declan," she murmured, her fingers running through his longer hair. She stood on her toes and ran her lips over his unkempt beard. "No. I called myself foolish. Never you."

"What?" he whispered.

She cupped his face, holding him in as an implacable hold as he

191

held her. "I realized I'd been such a fool to ever doubt you. To ever worry whether you loved me." Her gaze held a deep sorrow. "Then you ran away, and the doubts assailed me again."

"Oh, my love," Declan whispered, as he ran his fingers over her silky cheek. "I swear I love you. I hoped you could come to love me when I finished building your new store." She shook her head, and the hope in his gaze dimmed. "Nay?" he rasped. "It won't be enough?" He let out a deep breath. "Tell me what I have to do, Lo. I'll do it."

"*Shh*," she whispered, her eyes full of compassion. "Don't beg," she pleaded, resting her head against his chest and kissing the underside of his jaw.

His breath hitched in and out of him. "For you, I will." He attempted to step away from her, but she clung to him like a burr.

"I will not let you run away again, my Declan," she vowed. "I will not let you misinterpret what I mean again." She held on tight, as she waited for him to meet her fervent gaze. "There is nothing you have to do to earn my love, for you already have it. If this all burned down tonight and if the crates of books were thrown into the Missouri, it would not lessen my love for you."

"Lo," he rasped, as he ran a hand down her long neck to her shoulder.

"I love you, Declan, as you are. You are a wonderful father, son, brother." She stood on her toes again, kissing him softly. "And husband."

He stared at her with a regret-filled gaze. "I haven't been a good husband to you these past weeks."

She covered his lips with her fingers, shaking her head as she smiled at him. "No, beloved, don't dwell on our misunderstanding." She swallowed. "Promise me that, in the future, you'll talk with me and trust me with your fears."

He kissed her fingers, whispering, "I promise." He paused as he stared deeply into her eyes. "I promise to believe in us. To honor you. And to cherish this love that is growing between us."

She cupped his face. "Oh, Declan, I do too." She glanced around the half-built building. "Together I know we will have the most wondrous life, sharing it all with Gavin."

"Ah, love, of that I have no doubt."

~

Read on for a Sneak Peek at Maggie and Dunmore's story, *Pioneer Devotion.* Order Now and Available in May 2021!

SNEAK PEEK AT PIONEER DEVOTION!

Fort Benton, Montana Territory, June 1868

"*Stay away from my daughter.*"

The words repeated again and again in Dunmore's mind as he stared at his horses while they plodded along the primitive wagon road that would return him to Fort Benton. He ignored the prattling of the man beside him who was desperate to return to civilization and leave the wilds of the Territory behind him. Dunmore suspected the man had beggared himself rather than earning the riches he'd imagined. His coach was full of such men and he knew he'd have a busy season ferrying men around the Territory. None of that mattered now.

The momentary respite of thinking of something other than Seamus O'Rourke's edict ended as he again thought about the conversation he'd had with the man before leaving his hometown of Fort Benton a few weeks ago. Somehow, Seamus had learned of his passionate embrace with his youngest daughter, Maggie. After years of patience on Dunmore's part, Seamus had extracted a promise of more time.

He grunted in disbelief. "More time," he muttered. If there was one thing he never took for granted, it was the guarantee for more time. He sat in disillusioned silence as images of his beloved Maggie filled his vision. Her impish smile. Her eyes gleaming with triumph when she found a successful treatment to help a family member who was ailing. The warm glow in her gaze as she stared at him. Taking a deep breath, he banished his memories of their embrace. Of her kisses. He knew if he thought of them, he'd never honor his promise.

He only hoped Maggie would understand.

Order Now! Pioneer Devotion Available to Read May 2021!

RAMONA'S READER'S NOTE

It was a roller coaster of a ride writing this novel, as I brought back a beloved character from the Banished Saga. Mr. Pickens was a wise old man in that series, and during a brainstorming session with my dad, he had the brilliant idea of bringing Mr. Pickens back. He didn't have to twist my arm, as Mr. Pickens had always been one of my favorite characters. Now, in the O'Rourke Saga, he's a much younger man, and it was so much fun writing Mr. Pickens as a man in his thirties. It was also one of the last brilliant ideas my dad shared with me before he passed away, so it's a precious memory for me. I hope you enjoyed Mr. Pickens as much as I enjoyed writing him.

Thank you, dear reader, for your emails, messages and never-ending enthusiasm for the books I write. None of this would be possible without you and I am incredibly grateful.

Don't forget to join my newsletter to stay up to date with releases and news about my life in Montana!

My family is always interested in all that I do and are my greatest champions. Thank you for cheering me on, especially when I'm having days when I am floundering.

Thank you, DB, for you boundless support and enthusiasm for all of my projects. You're such a great cheerleader- thank you!

Thank you, Jenny Q, for another amazing cover!

ALSO BY RAMONA FLIGHTNER

The O'Rourke Family Montana Saga

Follow the O'Rourke Family as they settle in Fort Benton, Montana Territory in 1860's.

Sign up here to receive the prequel, *Pioneer Adventure* to the new Saga as a thank you for subscribing to my newsletter!

Pioneer Adventure (Prequel)

Pioneer Dream (OFMS, Book 1)- Kevin and Aileen

Pioneer Desire- (OFMS, Book 2)- Ardan and Deirdre

Pioneer Yearning- (OFMS, Book 3) Niamh and Cormac

Pioneer Longing (OFMS, Book 4)- Eamon and Phoebe

Pioneer Bliss (OFMS, Book 5) Declan and Lorena

Pioneer Devotion (OFMS, Book 6) Maggie and Dunmore- Coming Soon!

Bear Grass Springs Series

Never fear, I am busy at work on the next book in the series! If you want to make sure you never miss a release, a special, a cover reveal, or a short story just for my fans, sign up for my newsletter!

Immerse yourself in 1880's Montana as the MacKinnon siblings and their extended family find love!

Montana Untamed (BGS, Book 1) Cailean and Annabelle

Montana Grit (BGS, Book 2) Alistair and Leticia

Montana Maverick (BGS, Book 3) Ewan and Jessamine

Montana Renegade(BGS, Book 4) Warren and Helen

Jubilant Montana Christmas (BGS, Book 5) Leena and Karl

Montana Wrangler (BGS, Book 6) Sorcha and Frederick

Unbridled Montana Passion (BGS, Book 7) Fidelia and Bears

Montana Vagabond (BGS, Book 8) Jane and Ben

Exultant Montana Christmas (BGS, Book 9) Ewan and Jessamine

Lassoing a Montana Heart, (BGS, Book 10)- Slims and Davina

Healing Montana Love (BGS Book 11)- Dalton and Charlotte

Runaway Montana Groom (BGS, Book 12) Peter and Philomena- Coming Soon!

Substitute Montana Bride (BGS Book 13) Coming in 2021!

The Banished Saga

Follow the McLeod, Sullivan and Russell families as they find love, their loyalties are tested, and they overcome the challenges of their time. A sweeping saga set between Boston and Montana in early 1900's America.

The Banished Saga: (In Order)

Love's First Flames (Prequel)

Banished Love (Banished Saga, Book One)

Reclaimed Love (Banished Saga, Book Two)

Undaunted Love(Banished Saga, Book Three) (Part One)

Undaunted Love (Banished Saga, Book Three) (Part Two)

Tenacious Love (Banished Saga, Book Four)

Unrelenting Love (Banished Saga, Book Five)

Escape To Love (Banished Saga, Book Six)

Resilient Love (Banished Saga, Book Seven)

Abiding Love (Banished Saga, Book Eight)

Triumphant Love (Banished Saga, Book Nine)

ABOUT THE AUTHOR

Ramona is a historical romance author who loves to immerse herself in research as much as she loves writing. A native of Montana, every day she marvels that she gets to live in such a beautiful place. When she's not writing, her favorite pastimes are fly fishing the cool clear streams of a Montana river, hiking in the mountains, and spending time with family and friends.

Ramona's heroines are strong, resilient women, the type of women you'd love to have as your best friend. Her heroes are loyal and honorable, men you'd love to meet or bring home to introduce to your family for Sunday dinner. She hopes her stories bring the past alive and allow you to forget the outside world for a while.

BB bookbub.com/authors/ramona-flightner
instagram.com/rflightner
facebook.com/authorramonaflightner
goodreads.com/ramonaflightner
pinterest.com/Ramonaauthor